A Dangerous Game

JULIA TEMPLETON

Cerridwen Press

What the critics are saying...

∽

4 hearts! "What an extremely entertaining story!! Ms. Templeton certainly knows how to write a steamy and highly erotic historical romance. She infuses it with two dynamic lead characters plus a myriad of secondary ones. The story never falters as Ms. Templeton takes us on a ride as we watch Salvatore and Nicolette's exploration of their "new" relationship. Once again, Ms. Templeton has done a great job of merging a historical romance with just enough erotic action to give it some sizzle!" ~ *Love Romances*

"Templeton is a fabulous writer of historical romance! *A Dangerous Game* is a page-turning romantic read which you will find impossible to put down. Featuring a likable heroine, a sexy hero and a narrative which will grip you from the very first sentence, this is one fabulous historical romance which should be on everyone's keeper shelves!" ~ *ECataRomance Reviews*

"This story reminds me a lot of Barbara Cartland's books. As a big fan of Barbara Cartland's books, it always left me a little bit unsatisfied. Virgin meets rogue — you can foresee the end but now reading *A Dangerous Game* finally I could read what Mrs. Cartland forgot to write about. I loved the writing style of MS.TEMPLETON. The storyline and the steamy love scenes will leave you breathless. I can't wait to read more of MS. TEMPLETON's books." ~ *Cupid's Library Reviews*

"*A Dangerous Game* is about playing with emotions and having them backfire on you. *A Dangerous Game* is sweet, sensuous and romantic. I enjoyed reading about two people who suddenly become blindingly aware of each other after such a long friendship. I also liked how the book did not go the way I expected it to. That is refreshing. *A Dangerous Game* is all about not knowing who you are going to fall in love with until it happens and how you handle the fall. It is an enjoyable, lighthearted read." ~ *Fallen Angels Reviews*

"Ms. Templeton's writing is top caliber and a must read for readers who enjoy the historical romance genre...I didn't want this beautiful novel to end. I'm of the opinion that for years to come *A Dangerous Game* will live on in the memory of readers." ~ *Novelspot Reviews*

A Cerridwen Press Publication

www.cerridwenpress.com

A Dangerous Game

ISBN 9781419954290
ALL RIGHTS RESERVED.
A Dangerous Game Copyright © 2005 Julia Templeton
Edited by Pamela Cohen.
Cover art by Syneca.

This book printed in the U.S.A. by Jasmine–Jade Enterprises, LLC.

Electronic book Publication September 2005
Trade paperback Publication February 2007

Cerridwen Press is an imprint of Ellora's Cave Publishing, Inc.®

Also by Julia Templeton

୬

If you are interested in a spicier read (and are over 18), check out the author's erotic romances at Ellora's Cave Publishing (www.ellorascave.com).

Chances Are (*anthology*)

Dangerous Desire

Hometown Hero

Kieran the Black

Masquerade

Now and Forever

About the Author

୬

Julia Templeton has written contemporary, historical and time-travel romances for Cerridwen Press and other magazines and book publishers, and romantica for Ellora's Cave Publishing. She also pens novels under the pseudonym Anastasia Black with writing partner and fellow Ellora's Cave author Tracy Cooper-Posey. Aside from her passion for writing, Julia also enjoys reading, listening to music, collecting research books, traveling and spending time with family.

Julia welcomes comments from readers. You can find her website and email address on her author bio page at www.cerridwenpress.com.

Tell Us What You Think

We appreciate hearing reader opinions about our books. You can email us at Comments@EllorasCave.com.

A DANGEROUS GAME

ॐ

Dedication

෨

This book is dedicated to Donna Chase, the best mother-in-law on the planet. Thanks for your love and support, but even more, thanks for having such an incredible son☺. We both miss you!

Special thanks to Aaron Meyer, Rock Violinist extraordinaire. You're an amazingly talented musician, and I'm so thrilled with the success you've achieved.

It's well deserved, my friend.

Chapter One

London, 1819

ॐ

The moment was at hand.

Nicolette glanced at Salvatore, her partner and best friend, pretending she didn't feel the piercing eyes of two hundred and thirty-seven aristocrats on her.

"The world-renowned musicians—Salvatore Casale and Nicolette Rockwell!" The footman's voice reverberated off the high ceiling of the ballroom.

Nicolette squared her shoulders as whispers spread quickly throughout the room. She knew what they said. She and Salvatore were by-blows of wealthy English lords, mistakes to be locked away forever. True, she may be a marquess's bastard, but she was wealthy, and she had done it all on her own with no help from the father who'd turned his back on her the day she was born.

And why should she care what *the ton* thought of her? After all, her gown was made from as fine a silk as any of the other women present. Her hair glimmered with diamonds, a gift from one of her many admirers who refused to take back the beautiful gems.

Releasing an unsteady breath, Nicolette took everything in. The long, narrow ballroom, the musicians playing on the elaborate stage, London's elite spread out beneath four enormous gold-plated chandeliers. She scanned the crowd, looking for the man she must enchant. A man who must become so enamored of her, he would risk everything—even marriage to the greatest heiress in all of England.

She nodded at the people they passed, watching as women whispered behind their fans, their eyes not wavering from Salvatore, her incredibly handsome friend. Salvatore had an exotic quality, rare in men. His beauty drew women like moths to a flame. His long, dark hair shone brilliantly under the lights, his golden eyes framed by long, black lashes, which Nicolette teased belonged on a woman instead of a man. Those light eyes could hypnotize any woman. Even when he was young, his power over the opposite sex had been obvious.

"There he is. In the doorway, the tall one," Salvatore said, his voice unusually tense, his hold on her tightening.

Nicolette followed his gaze to a set of double doors off to the right. Her heart skittered at her first glimpse of Darian Tremayne, Earl of Kedgwick. Short, brown hair framed arresting features; square jaw, aquiline nose, and dark eyes — eyes the same shape as Salvatore's.

In his hand he held a glass, and as he brought it to his lips, his eyes met hers over the rim. Her stomach clenched in a tight knot. He was more striking than she had imagined. Her confidence wavered. She glanced at the women who clustered nearby, their gazes smoldering as they stared at the powerful man who seemed aware of their scrutiny, his gaze flitting over them in a callous way that made her blood run cold.

"Do not be too obvious," Salvatore's voice broke into her thoughts. "Men enjoy the chase. He is watching our every move, so it is apparent he is taken with you."

All her life she'd heard of Darian Tremayne, Salvatore's older, *legitimate* brother. Salvatore resented the man who'd been lavished with their father's wealth, title and attention, while he and his mother had been abandoned and left to starve on the streets of London.

"Look, here comes his bride-to-be."

Nicolette's gaze followed Salvatore's to a petite blonde making her way toward Darian. Dressed in a mignonette-green ball gown with satin trimmings and puffed sleeves,

Elizabeth Dutton, the daughter of the Duke of Durham, with her pinched features and beady eyes could not be considered a beauty by any means…which made things easier for Nicolette and her mission.

During the next hour Nicolette mingled and danced, while keeping an eye on Darian as he played the perfect gentleman to his fiancée. Elizabeth appeared completely enamored of her future husband, if her vibrant smile and robust laughter were any indication.

They were perfectly suited. Wealthy beyond measure, Darian and Elizabeth had never wanted for anything in their lives, which meant these two incredibly spoiled individuals wholeheartedly deserved each other. While they had been pampered, she had lived a life of poverty, sharing a lumpy cot with Salvatore, while listening to the sounds of whores pleasuring their patrons. Their only escape had been music.

"It appears our fun has ended for now. We are being summoned by Lady Perrin." Salvatore motioned toward their vivacious host, a rotund woman known for her heavy drinking and loose tongue.

Nicolette took a deep, calming breath as they made their way through the crowd to the stage. Though she had played before kings and queens and not suffered from nerves, tonight was different. She needed to enchant Darian Tremayne, to seduce him right beneath his fiancée's nose. Elizabeth's father, a man known for his strict moral code, had made it perfectly clear that Darian, a rakehell with a penchant for voluptuous actresses, was to remain faithful to his wife-to-be. Any indiscretion and the wedding would be called off.

As Nicolette took her place at the piano, she ran her fingers lightly over the familiar keys. She smiled softly, feeling the tension slowly fade. The piano was like an old friend. At the lowest point of her life it had become her salvation, and she owed it all to Salvatore. He'd taught her how to play— how to feel every chord to the very depths of her soul. She nodded at her partner, who stood with violin at the ready.

Their gazes locked. Salvatore smiled softly, she began to play, and as always, her eyes closed of their own accord as she gave herself over to the music.

* * * * *

Salvatore watched Darian, who stood apart from the crowd, leaning against the back wall, a drink in hand. *His brother*, the esteemed Earl of Kedgwick. The man who had been blessed with legitimacy.

Already Darian was captivated with Nicolette. From the moment they had started to play, his brother had not moved a muscle, his gaze riveted on her. Salvatore knew the look in the other man's eyes—desire. He had grown accustomed to the attention directed at Nicolette since she had matured into a young woman. Now it appeared that even his brother was not immune to her charms.

If Nicolette could stop Darian's upcoming marriage, then he would have the revenge he had dreamed of since his father abandoned him and his mother. Word had it the old bastard, while on his deathbed, made Darian promise he would marry the Duke of Durham's daughter, Elizabeth, thereby joining together two of the most influential families of *the ton*.

Salvatore smiled to himself, imagining his father rolling over in his grave when that union did not take place—and how furious the countess would be when the Kedgwick name was once again scandalized.

Salvatore glanced to Darian's right, to Elizabeth. For an instant she looked away, but then peeked his way again. Salvatore held her gaze and she shifted, a blush racing from her neck to her cheeks. He smiled at the woman before turning toward Nicolette whose eyes were still closed.

How striking his Nic was. Her beautiful, classic features had been the inspiration behind many of the scores he'd written. How lost he would be without her in his world.

Together they had conquered Europe, playing in every large city to a full house.

It seemed like yesterday she'd wore her hair plaited and raced about in boys' clothing. Overnight she had blossomed into a striking woman that made men stop and stare. Waist-length, silky auburn curls that floated when she walked had replaced the braids of her youth. Long, thick lashes framed her large, green, almond-shaped eyes. She had a small upturned nose, high cheekbones, full lips, and a long, slender neck, which gave way to full breasts that made her small waist appear even tinier. Indeed, Nicolette had no idea of her power over the opposite sex.

Lord help him when she did.

As though sensing his gaze, Nicolette opened her eyes, and her lips curved into a soft smile. His heart warmed with love for this woman who was partner, friend and constant companion.

She never complained about the tedious life they lived, the constant traveling, the constant entertaining, the constant practice and push to do better. Already they had been accepted into all the finest homes of Europe's aristocrats. Though they were wealthier than they'd ever dreamed, this life was not for the faint of heart, and he wondered if, like him, she yearned for a life of stability.

* * * * *

Nicolette couldn't stop trembling. As Salvatore steered her past the swelling crowd and out the double doors onto the veranda, she tried to convince herself she had iron control over her emotions. Yet, with every passing moment, it was obvious that she was not as prepared to seduce Darian Tremayne as she'd thought. She must gather her thoughts and remember her focus.

"He could not take his eyes from you the entire time. You should have seen his face. He was clearly mesmerized."

Salvatore's smile was triumphant as he looked down at her. "This is proving to be easier than I imagined."

"I am not so sure I can do this."

He lifted her chin with gentle fingers. "I would never force you to do something you do not want to do. If you desire, we can leave now and never look back."

She met his unwavering gaze and knew he meant every word. Salvatore would never hurt her—or make her do anything against her will. He had been her only family since her mother's death nine years ago. Since that time, he'd supported her in everything she'd chosen to do, and now it was her time to pay him back for all he'd done. She sighed heavily. "I'm fine. My confidence is just beginning to waver."

The words brought a renewed smile to Salvatore's lips. "Nic, you are the most beautiful woman here, and it is common knowledge Darian Tremayne cannot resist a gorgeous woman, particularly an auburn-haired, green-eyed Venus."

She rolled her eyes. "You forget I am immune to your charm."

He laid a hand over his heart and attempted to appear hurt, but failed miserably. "I am serious, Nic. Truly, you have more fire in you than any other woman. A man would be a fool to deny you."

If only she had Salvatore's confidence. "I certainly hope you are right."

"You are ever the courageous one," he said with a light laugh, hugging her to him.

She rested her head against his shoulder, taking the comfort that only he could give. How many times had he been there for her? All her life she'd been able to rely on only one person, and that was Salvatore. Only he knew the hell her life had been. A life as a bastard, always watching those fortunate souls of *the ton* who held the titles, the wealth, the prestige—

while she and Salvatore had lived in a shabby brothel, eating scraps, yearning for the day they would escape.

"Please forgive us. We did not mean to interrupt."

The deep voice startled Nicolette out of her thoughts. She turned to find Darian Tremayne and his fiancée watching her and Salvatore intently.

Nicolette's pulse skittered to have the man she was to seduce, standing before her in the flesh. A shadow fell across his face, hiding all but his dark eyes, which held her pinned to the spot. The hair on the back of her neck stood on end. It seemed at that moment he could see all the way to her soul.

"You did not interrupt us," Salvatore said, breaking the awkward silence. Releasing Nicolette, he stepped forward and lifted Elizabeth's hand to his lips. "Lady Elizabeth, it is an honor to meet you at long last."

The woman's cheeks blazed crimson.

Salvatore glanced at his brother. "And you as well, Lord Kedgwick."

Darian's arrogant gaze shifted from Nicolette to Salvatore, his lips quirking in a sly smile. How she yearned to slap that smile clean off his face.

"You were exceptional," Darian said, his gaze returning to hers, before dropping to the low décolletage of her gown.

At her side Salvatore straightened and cleared his throat. "Thank you, my lord."

Elizabeth stared at Salvatore. "You are most talented."

"Thank you, Lady Elizabeth," Salvatore replied, pulling Nicolette up against him.

Darian finally turned his attention to Salvatore. "Have we met before? You look familiar."

Doing his best to look perplexed, Salvatore shook his head. "I doubt it. Nicolette and I grew up in London, but I have to believe we frequented different establishments than you."

"Perhaps you played at White's?"

Salvatore shook his head. "Never."

"Watiers'?"

"Sorry. We have not been in London for years. We've spent most of our time in France."

Darian's gaze strayed to the large windows where couples danced by. "Elizabeth was just telling me that she would love to dance with you."

Elizabeth frowned up at her intended. "I did?"

Darian nodded.

"Would you do me the honor of joining me for a dance?" Salvatore asked, dropping Nicolette's hand and extending his arm for the duke's daughter.

Nicolette watched in strained silence as the two disappeared into the throng of dancers, ever aware of the earl's dark eyes assessing her. In all her eighteen years, she had never been so nervous. Being an entertainer, she had never been the quiet type, and always adapted to any given situation. But this was not just any given situation.

"Tell me, Miss—"

"Nicolette."

He smiled as though amused, obviously unaccustomed to women using their Christian name. No doubt he thought her unladylike for doing so. "Very well...*Nicolette*, who taught you to play like that?"

The way he said her name was almost like a caress. No doubt he used that voice often to get his way. His tone annoyed her. "Salvatore taught me."

A dark brow lifted in surprise. "Truly?"

She nodded, wishing Salvatore would hurry up and make his way back to her. "He plays several instruments, quite brilliantly, in fact. The violin is his favorite. One day he was working on a score, and he asked for my help. I caught on quickly and from that moment on, I knew I wanted to be a musician."

His gaze once again strayed to her neckline. "It is obvious you enjoy what you do."

"Indeed, I am most fortunate," she replied, glancing past him, hoping to see Salvatore walking her way. She saw him on the dance floor and smiled. There was an elegance about Salvatore that many men lacked. Perhaps it was his musical background that gave him the gift to dance better than most. Whatever it was, he had the ability to draw women to wherever they went. In fact, even from where Nicolette stood, she could see the clusters of women watching him, wanting him.

"Are you in London for long?" Darian asked, bringing Nicolette's attention back to him. His gaze was so intense she shifted on her feet. She could not wait to escape this man. If only there was another way.

"I can not say for certain. We have several engagements, but Salvatore does not like to stay in one place for long. He bores easily."

"And you." His gaze wandered down her length, assessing her like she was prized horseflesh. "Do you become bored as well?"

She bit into her lower lip, fighting the urge to tell him exactly what she thought of him and his too-intimate stare. "At times I become bored, but not nearly as much as Salvatore."

"Is he your lover?"

His abrupt question made her falter. She opened her mouth to respond, but no words came out.

He laughed, but it didn't seem to reach his eyes. "I did not mean to offend."

Now she could add liar to his list of faults, because he most certainly had meant to offend. She squared her shoulders. Who did he think he was? Just because he was part of the aristocracy didn't mean he could ask her such an intimate question. He would have never been so bold with any other woman present. But she was a bastard, and therefore, rude questions could be asked without thought of consequence. In his world, she was beneath him—a servant, a mere musician, meant for his amusement.

With a flick of her wrist, she opened her fan to cool her heated cheeks, hoping that she at least appeared composed when she felt anything but. "My private life is none of your concern." Revenge or no revenge, if she stayed a moment longer in his company she would surely say something she'd regret. Her heart hammered against her ribs as she walked past him.

He grabbed her wrist lightly, and she stopped to face him. His arrogant grin faded as his gaze slipped to her chest again. When his thumb skimmed over her erratic pulse, she pulled away.

"It was a pleasure to meet you," he said, his voice low and intent.

Unable to stand the predatory gleam in his eye a moment longer, Nicolette turned on her heel and left him staring after her. She could feel his gaze burning into her back. To add to her fury, she heard his laughter all the way back to the ballroom.

* * * * *

Salvatore watched the exchange going on outside between Darian and Nicolette as closely as one could while dancing in a room with hundreds of people, and making every effort to be attentive to his dance partner.

Nicolette's shoulders were rigid, her chin lifted. Salvatore knew that angry stance well.

It took all the willpower he possessed not to storm outside and demand to know what Darian had said to upset her so. Instead, he watched helplessly as Darian in turn looked after Nicolette, who reached the ballroom, only to have a group of eager young men converge on her. With a charming smile, she took the arm of a boy who looked fresh out of boarding school, and practically floated to the dance floor. Her laughter was light, like the chime of a bell, and he found himself smiling, relieved to find her anger short-lived.

"Salvatore, tell me about your life."

Salvatore turned to Elizabeth. "I would hate to bore you when we could be doing other things."

Her throat convulsed as she swallowed hard. "Other things?"

He grinned, actually feeling sympathetic toward the young woman who would marry a man who would never be faithful to her. "Yes, like dancing and enjoying the fabulous music."

The music ended a moment later and Salvatore breathed a sigh of relief. He took Elizabeth by the hand, bringing it to his lips, kissing the skin covered by her glove, before folding it in the crook of his arm. She flushed and he noted her fingers curled tightly around his elbow. "What a wonderful dance partner you have been," he said, meaning it. Though far from beautiful, Elizabeth had been schooled by the best tutors in London, and she knew her way around a dance floor.

"It has been a delight, Lady Elizabeth." Releasing her hand, he turned to Darian. "And it was a pleasure meeting you as well, Lord Kedgwick."

Darian merely nodded, his gaze shifting to something over Salvatore's shoulder. He had been excused, already forgotten. Too below Kedgwick to give him another moment's notice.

Oh how the mighty will fall.

Salvatore turned on his heel and started toward Nicolette. He found her dancing with a gangly youth who was stepping all over her slippered feet, but she smiled and chatted with him.

He smiled inwardly, proud of the young woman she had become. He had never met another person so talented, so kind and so giving. For over a decade they had lived together, four of those years alone...after the death of his mother. Though it had just been the two of them, they functioned like any family—watching out for each other, and loving each other. Often times he still treated her like a child and he had to catch himself, realizing that she was a woman now.

When the dance ended, Salvatore walked out to meet her, taking her hand in his, and placing the other on her tiny waist. "How did it go with Kedgwick, or need I ask?"

"He thinks you and I are lovers. He said as much."

He nearly laughed aloud, but seeing her discomfort, he refrained. Did she not know that everyone believed they were lovers? After all, society did not take kindly to two people of the opposite sex living together—particularly *unmarried* people who continually thumbed their nose at convention and did what they wanted, when they wanted, and made no apologies.

"That is absolute rubbish," he replied, holding her tighter. Even now he could see others watching the two of them. No one else in the room held each other so close. He glanced at Darian, to find him among the audience, scowling. So, Darian was jealous, was he? No doubt his brother wished he could hold Nicolette as tightly, or as intimately as he did now. For a moment he gloried in his small victory. The other man yearned for what Salvatore had.

Excellent.

"I didn't expect him to be so...attractive. True, his nose is a bit too large for his face, but his eyes and lips are very nice." Nicolette released a long-winded sigh. "What if I fall in love with him?"

Salvatore's stomach rolled. He stopped in midstep and looked into her eyes. Relief washed over him seeing that she was trying to refrain from laughing, but without success.

Jest or no jest, he wondered why he had never considered that Nicolette might *actually* find Darian attractive. What if she did fall in love with him? Women loved harder than men. Once they became intimate with a man, they wanted his heart as well. His mind raced with the possibility. What if Nic lost her heart to Darian, and what if Darian fell hopelessly in love with Nicolette?

Nicolette lifted a finely shaped brow. "What's the matter?"

"What do you mean?"

"You're frowning."

He shook his head. "It must have been the wine. I have a headache."

Concern flashed in her eyes and she put a hand to his brow. She always turned maternal toward him when he complained of the slightest ailment, acting more like a mother than his own ever had. "Perhaps we should take our leave."

They had stopped in the middle of the floor, amidst the dancers who all turned to look at them.

Nicolette seemed not to notice. Instead, she took him by the hand and led him off the dance floor. "Let's go home, and put you to bed."

Salvatore followed behind Nicolette. He glanced over at Darian, and noted that his brother did not look happy in the least. If he was not mistaken, that was jealousy in the other man's dark eyes.

Chapter Two

One Week Later

Kedgwick Hall – The Engagement Party

ℰᴑ

"There it is, Kedgwick Hall," Salvatore said, his voice missing its usual zeal. Nicolette guessed the cause. This was his first glimpse of his ancestral home.

Nicolette set her book aside and looked out the window. The enormous three-story structure built of dark gray stone seemed out of place in the serene countryside. It had been built to take one's breath away, and the architect had succeeded in doing so by adding an elaborate wrought iron gate embellished with gold that, at the moment, was being opened by uniformed guards.

And all this luxury belonged to the Earl of Kedgwick, Darian Tremayne.

The very man she must seduce this week.

How she despised the arrogant man.

She must appear calm and composed. Since meeting Darian last weekend, she had slept very little, her mind too occupied with ways to lure him.

As the carriage came to a stop before the entrance staircase, Salvatore sat forward. "Well, it looks like the game is about to begin."

"Indeed," she replied with a forced smile, willing the butterflies in her stomach to stop.

As Salvatore exited the coach, Nicolette inhaled a deep breath and took the hand of the footman who stood at the ready. Once her feet were firmly planted on the ground, Nicolette looked up at the stone manor where Corinthian pilasters stood below a flat roof. An enormous flag of the family's coat-of-arms waved proudly in the wind.

Walking up the steps Nicolette could see Salvatore's demeanor slip further. No doubt he wondered what it would have been like to have inherited his father's home and title. She, for one, was grateful her father had not acknowledged her. Her life had not been entirely bad. In fact, she at least had the freedom to make her own choices from an early age— something unheard of for a woman. There would be no arranged marriage for her, no life full of needlepoint and tea parties, where a husband dictated everything she did.

She shivered at the thought of marrying for money and prominence instead of love, which in turn made Nicolette wonder if Elizabeth truly loved Darian. Despite the sidelong glances she threw Salvatore last weekend, it certainly seemed as though Elizabeth were besotted with her intended.

Poor thing.

Thoughts of Elizabeth evaporated when the manor's entry doors opened and an elegantly dressed footman wearing powdered wig and too much rouge bowed to the floor. Nicolette looked past the servant to the foyer with its stark marble columns, and the sweeping staircase made of dark, polished wood, which gleamed under the sun filtering through the skylight overhead.

An aging butler approached. His weathered face speaking of his advanced years, his smile warm and genuine as he bowed stiffly. "Good afternoon, Mr. Casale and Miss Rockwell, your rooms are ready for you. Will you please follow me?"

The butler's slow gait allowed her time to take in the surroundings. Her fingers skimmed the polished banister as they ascended the staircase to the second floor where pictures of Kedgwick ancestors hung. She noted how Salvatore's gaze skipped over the portraits quickly, finally settling on the one of his father sitting beside a stern-faced brunette, and a young boy sitting at their feet—Darian, the late earl and his countess. The countess paled in comparison to Salvatore's mother, a woman of Greek descent, and a daughter of gypsies who enjoyed dancing for her lovers. The earl had adored her...until she became pregnant with Salvatore.

The butler stopped before a cherrywood door and opened it. "Miss Rockwell, a footman will be along with your bags shortly." He turned and opened the door across the hall. "Mr. Casale, this is your room."

With a promise to see Salvatore soon, Nicolette shut the door behind her and took in her surroundings. The room was spacious and warm, with a fire already blazing in the grate. The white marble fireplace was a work of art in itself. The smiling cherubs and gold embellishments must have cost a small fortune.

The large bed was canopied, with white gossamer panels surrounding it. There was a wardrobe, one high-backed chair, a gorgeous light blue velvet settee, vanity, and assorted tables where vases of freshly cut flowers set, filling the room with their scent.

Crossing the room, she threw open the balcony doors and was met by a setting that would make any gardener green with envy. There were manicured hedges along graveled paths, rose bushes of every color, and an enormous fountain in a courtyard where statues stood in each corner. Nicolette leaned on the wrought iron railing, taking in the splendor. Poor Salvatore...he had been deprived of such a beautiful home.

With her partner uppermost in mind, Nicolette went to him.

His room was as large as hers, yet instead of feminine touches, it was filled with heavy furniture made of dark wood. Amongst such finery sat Salvatore, sitting as still as the statues that graced the courtyard. He didn't bother to turn when she closed the door behind her. She walked to him and without looking at her; he reached out and took hold of her hand, his long fingers curling around hers.

"What's wrong?" she asked, even though she knew the answer. His hatred toward his father would never leave him. Being in the man's home would make the week ahead most difficult.

He glanced up at her, and the pain reflected in his eyes made her heart lurch. "I hate that my anger nearly strangles me every time I play a private party. Now that I am in *his* home, it is even worse. The bastard! How I wish I could have met him. I would have loved to have seen his face when I told him I was his son. The son of the woman he had pledged his love to, then turned into a whore."

She squeezed his hand, hoping for the words to ease the hurt. "You are better off having not known him."

He laughed sardonically. "Yes, I would much rather be a struggling musician for the rest of my life, than be a wealthy lord who spends the day frolicking with friends." He ran his free hand through his hair. "I wish I had your courage, your ability to forgive."

"You know, we are hardly struggling. In truth, it could be worse."

He smiled then, his white teeth flashing, and he even chuckled.

"See, I knew you could not stay all gloom and doom for long."

A soft knock on the door brought him to his feet. He kissed her hand before releasing it. "That would be our bags." He took a deep breath. "And I am quite finished feeling sorry for myself."

She laughed, relieved. "Thank God!"

He was almost to the door when he turned. "Perhaps we shall be fortunate enough to run into the lord of the manor."

"Perhaps," she replied, hoping that Darian had decided to skip his own engagement party.

* * * * *

An hour later Nicolette had still not seen Darian or Elizabeth.

Instead, she and Salvatore had managed to get themselves involved in a competitive round of croquet, which, at the moment, she was in danger of winning.

Though she usually ignored gossip, she found that the loose-lipped Lady Mariweather, a beautiful widow at the age of thirty, had more than a few tidbits to share regarding the previous earl.

"The man's appetite for women and gambling put him out of favor with *the ton*," Lady Mariweather said under her breath as she delicately hit the ball, scarcely moving it from its previous position.

Salvatore leaned on his mallet. "Surely he wasn't as bad as that? After all, most men take mistresses."

"Please, call me Charlotte." She laughed and playfully hit Salvatore on the arm, her gloved hand lingering on his biceps. "Oh, my dear, man, of course all men cheat, but the earl had the audacity to attend a soiree with a woman on each arm—two actresses who were young enough to be his daughters. Fortunately, his wife was away on holiday in Paris but a friend was present, and she immediately wrote the countess. By the time the countess arrived on English soil, the earl had managed to lose their London townhouse in a card game, had been challenged in two duels, one of which left him with an injured leg, along with an opium habit that rendered him unrecognizable."

Nicolette looked past Salvatore and Lady Mariweather to the lavish home and gardens. "If he squandered the family fortune, then how can his son afford to keep this fine home?"

Licking her lips, the widow leaned closer to Nicolette. "Well, after his father's death, Darian reinvested heavily in several ventures which did measurably well, but not well enough." She looked over her shoulder to make sure they were the only ones within hearing range. "Hence, the reason he is marrying the Duke of Durham's horse-faced daughter." Lady Mariweather snickered wickedly. "You may have already heard, but the Duke made sure that in the marriage contract Kedgwick would pledge his fidelity to Elizabeth and not stray. If he were to take a mistress or have a liaison, the marriage would be annulled and Kedgwick and his family would be ruined."

Nicolette met Salvatore's gaze. His lips quirked the slightest bit.

"Do you know that Kedgwick's mother has seen to it that only men attend her son?" She lowered her voice further. "Rather than have the temptation of a maid cleaning his quarters, a footman has the honor."

Doing his best to appear a tad sympathetic, Salvatore frowned. "Come, Charlotte, do you not feel a little sorry for the man?"

Charlotte sighed dramatically. "*The man* deserves everything he gets."

Salvatore lifted a brow. "You sound like a scorned lover."

Lady Mariweather flashed an innocent smile, her gaze shifting from his, down his long length and back again. "Why, my dear man, I do not know what you mean."

Annoyed by the blatant flirtation, Nicolette lifted her mallet, and slammed her ball into Salvatore's with enough force to send it sailing through the green lawns and into a thicket of deep brush. The small group of onlookers laughed in delight, and she smiled innocently as Salvatore glanced at her with brows lifted.

Walking toward the brush, he grinned devilishly and pushed up his sleeves, showing muscular forearms. A moment later he disappeared into the thick foliage. Nicolette was amazed Charlotte didn't follow him.

The ball shot out on the lawn, right in line with Lady Mariweather's. The buxom woman clapped her hands together, clearly delighted. "Oh, will you look, Salvatore, your ball is right next to mine!"

Excitement filled the air as Salvatore stepped out of the bushes, a confident smile on his face as he swung the mallet over his shoulder—a smile that quickly lost its luster.

Seeing where his gaze was directed, Nicolette turned and her breath caught in her throat.

Darian leaned against a tree, arms crossed over his wide chest, watching the game. His horse grazed nearby, his riding clothes evidence of where he had been this morning. Staring straight at her, he nodded in greeting. Nicolette gave a curt nod and quickly averted her gaze.

Damn, she'd hoped the man had been delayed, or found some other distraction to keep him from the party.

Salvatore's arm slipped about her waist. "Look who has finally joined the festivities?"

"So I see," she murmured.

"When the game is finished, perhaps he will come over and say hello."

"Salvatore, you are not going to hit me, are you?" Lady Mariweather said, her voice provocative. Apparently the older woman didn't like being left out of the conversation.

Salvatore flashed his most charming smile. "I would never hit you, Charlotte. Though I might just bang you."

Nicolette choked back a glib remark.

The widow bit into her lower lip.

Nauseated with the two, Nicolette put all her concentration into the game and within minutes the widow was out. Darian's gaze on her made her so unsettled that even when Salvatore tried to get her to smile, she scowled at him.

If only she could seduce Darian the way Charlotte seduced Salvatore, who even now stood at the sidelines, watching him like a bitch in heat. With a steadying breath, Nicolette swung and hit the ball, which in turn hit the stake, making her the winner. Applause sounded all around her, Salvatore's, as always, the loudest.

Salvatore kissed her hand, and she quickly pulled away. "I'm going to talk to him." Without awaiting his response, she walked straight for Darian, who at her approach, pushed away from the tree.

His gaze swept the length of her, lingering at her legs. She guessed he was not accustomed to women foregoing their undergarments, save for their shift, as was all the rage in Paris. Only on a warm day like today did she dare do so in England.

Now she wished she had piled on the petticoats, feeling naked as Darian's dark eyes burned with a fire she found unsettling.

How she yearned to be anywhere else.

"Lord Kedgwick," she said, stopping a few feet from him.

He stepped forward and reached for her hand. His thumb brushed over her knuckles before he kissed it. She wore no gloves, and again, she wished she would have, at least this once, followed decorum.

"Nicolette, what a pleasant surprise. I had no idea you would be attending the party. I must say your presence will make the week bearable." He finally released her hand.

"Your mother said our presence was to be a surprise."

"And what a nice surprise it is. In the space of a few moments my enthusiasm for the days ahead has increased tenfold."

Uncomfortable with his predatory gaze, she looked toward the manor. "Is your bride-to-be here yet?"

His smile quickly turned into a frown. "Lady Elizabeth is up at the house. She does not care to spend much time in the sun."

She glanced back at Salvatore. Though he conversed with a group of women, Lady Mariweather included, she could tell he watched her from the corner of his eye. If he could flirt, then so could she. She lifted her chin a fraction. "Does she not own a parasol?"

"The sun tires her," he said, taking a step closer. Every nerve in Nicolette's body told her to run as far and as fast as she could. *Do it for Salvatore.* With that single thought racing through her mind, she stood anchored to the spot, meeting his hot stare with one she hoped mirrored his.

Dear God this was harder than she'd thought it would be.

Nicolette arched a brow as she'd seen Lady Mariweather do moments before. "What a shame. It must be difficult when you like to spend time outdoors." She lifted her face and closed her eyes, stretching her neck in a way the heroine in one of her steamy novels did to gain a male admirer's attention. "I love the sun. I like when its rays cast a golden glow upon my skin."

When she opened her eyes, the heat she saw in the earl's dark gaze made her take a quick step back. "I could never understand why a woman should not be able to sport tan skin like a man. One appears so much healthier with a bronzed tone, do you not agree?"

He took another step toward her, forcing her to bend her head back to look at him. "It appears that you were born the wrong gender, Nicolette, for you yearn for a man's life."

She laughed, the sound more nervous than light. "A man's life, indeed. Yes, you are probably right. After all, it is the male heir who receives the title, the money, the honor, not to mention the home," she said, nodding toward the manor. "Yours, I might add, is quite extraordinary."

"How do you find your room?"

"My room is exquisite and the bed is very soft," she whispered.

His smile faded. "I would like to spend time with you this week…to make up for my lack of decorum on our last meeting. Perhaps we can—"

"Tell me, Kedgwick, do you wish to marry?"

He ran a hand through his hair, looked toward his grazing horse, then back at her. Still he said nothing.

"Your silence must mean you are uncertain. If you do not wish to marry, then why do you?"

His gaze locked with hers. "It is my duty."

"And will you take a lover?" she blurted, unable to keep the malice from her tone.

His look of shock lasted a brief moment, and then he laughed under his breath. "I do not pretend to know what will happen." His gaze wandered to the low décolletage of her gown. No doubt from his height he could see more than most.

Heat raced up her neck. She had to force herself not to cross her hands over her chest. "I would take lovers." She added the plural for emphasis.

He stepped toward her once again, and this time, reached out and slowly smoothed a wayward lock of hair behind her ear. His fingers lingered for a moment. "Would you now?" He was so close; their lips mere inches apart.

Nicolette took an abrupt step away, and hid her nervousness with a coy smile. *Where was Salvatore?* "If I did not desire to marry that person, then why should I *sleep* with only him for the rest of my life?"

"Do you think you will ever marry?"

She shrugged. "It depends."

"On?"

His brow furrowed. "If I fall in love."

He laughed, but it sounded forced. "Love is a fanciful notion, one that holds little precedence in marriage, particularly an arranged one."

"That is the difference between our worlds, Kedgwick. I should say on this particular occasion that I am the luckier one. Though you may have been brought up in wealth, and I in poverty, at least I am free to choose whom I so please."

"Then you are most fortunate."

She nodded. "Indeed, I am."

Darian glanced past her shoulder and frowned. "Look, here comes your lover now."

Before she could respond, Salvatore was at her side, putting an arm around her waist. Though she would never admit it to him, she was relieved he'd interrupted. He then turned and fixed her necklace, making sure the clasp fell to the back of her neck. The gesture was an intimate one, and Nicolette noted Darian's scowl as he watched them.

"We must have a rematch, my dear," Salvatore said, the hand that had been adjusting her necklace, now caressing her jaw, clearly in an effort to irritate his brother. "She is positively wicked at croquet, Kedgwick. You must play with her sometime."

"I have every intention of doing just that," Darian said, his words implying something other than playing croquet.

Salvatore straightened at his words, and lifted a dark brow. "Where is that little bride of yours?"

"Elizabeth is resting."

"Sorry to hear that," Salvatore answered, casually picking an imaginary string from the bodice of Nicolette's gown.

Darian appeared ready to come out of his skin. The nerve in his jaw jerked. "I'm sure Elizabeth will be delighted to see you both — if she decides to leave her room." His voice dripped with sarcasm.

Salvatore looked at the manor. "One can hardly blame her for holding up in her quarters in a home as grand as yours. You are a lucky man to have both a beautiful home and a beautiful fiancée."

"I am fortunate," Darian said, though his voice lacked conviction.

Salvatore nodded. "Fortunate — now that is an understatement." He looked down at Nicolette once again and they shared a smile. "Well, Nic, I suppose we should mingle with the other guests. There is a certain viscount who desires to meet you." He winked at her before he turned his attention to Darian. "It is good to see you again, Kedgwick. We look forward to the days ahead."

"As do I," Darian replied, his gaze fastening on Nicolette.

That dark stare said more than words ever could. He wanted her. Feeling sick to her stomach, Nicolette gladly took the hand Salvatore offered, and walked away.

Chapter Three

ഔ

It was early evening when Nicolette saw Darian again.

He stood outside on the veranda. It was a quiet night, the sky a dark gray. The light from a flickering flame cast a glow on the earl, who appeared completely at ease in the solitude.

For a moment Nicolette considered letting him be, but realizing it was a rare opportunity to be alone with him, she took a deep breath, pushed open the double doors and walked out.

Darian turned abruptly, his gaze sliding slowly down her body, reminding her yet again of his dangerous reputation as a rakehell. The earl's lovers were reported to be in the hundreds. How could one man who was still young, have made love to so many women? No wonder every time she saw him, he seemed to undress her with his eyes. Did that mean her attempt at seduction was working thus far?

"Nicolette, you are stunning as always."

At least he noticed her efforts, especially since the maid had worked tirelessly on styling her too-wavy hair, and the silk gown she wore had cost her a week's pay. "And you look handsome."

He seemed pleased by the compliment. "I was wondering if you would make it down for dinner tonight." His gaze slipped from hers, to the diamond necklace that rested near the swell of her breasts.

Did the man not realize how rude he was being, staring at her in such a way? He could at least attempt to be discreet, for goodness sake. "Why would I not attend?"

He shrugged. "I thought perhaps you would be too tired from your journey."

Despite the fact his gaze stayed riveted on her breasts, she managed to smile. "You forget that I am used to traveling. I enjoyed the trip since the weather was cooperative, and it gave me time to catch up on my reading."

His brows lifted.

"It surprises you that I can read?"

"A little."

What an arrogant ass he was. "Well, I will have you know I write poetry and music as well."

"I was not demeaning you in any way," he said, a sly smile on his face that completely contradicted his words. "I understand your life has not been an easy one, and I would never belittle a person for not having the same privileges as others. But I must say that I admire you...and Salvatore as well."

The anger she felt lessened under his thoughtful gaze and she tried to relax. "I did not come out here in search of compliments. I came to ask you if you would like to hear any particular song tonight. After all, the party is in your honor."

She saw the look of surprise flash in his eyes before he quickly masked it.

"You choose for me," he replied, taking a step toward her, pulling her roughly to him.

Every inch of his hard body was pressed flush against her, so close she could feel the pounding of his heart against her chest. He captured one of her hands within his own, and to her utter horror, he pulled it down to his manhood, pressing her hand against the hard ridge of his erection. "Feel what you do to me, Nicolette."

She was ready to scream when his mouth covered hers, his tongue thrusting past her lips.

"Darian, it is time for dinner!" a woman said from behind Nicolette.

Darian released her abruptly, his wild gaze shifting from her to his mother.

The countess glared at Nicolette, before she turned on her heel and went back inside.

Darian reached for her again, but Nicolette stepped back.

"Pick a song for me...just for me," he whispered, before heading in the direction his mother had gone.

* * * * *

Salvatore glanced up at the plaster ceiling with its three-dimensional images and wondered how much his great-great-grandfather had spent on the rendering. In his estimation, it had been far too much. His money would have been better spent on redecorating the all-pink drawing room's walls and furnishings, which had been overdone to the extreme.

Darian's mother approached Salvatore, her forced smile in place. "Salvatore, I believe your partner is out on the veranda with my son."

"Thank you, Lady Kedgwick," Salvatore replied with a curt nod, noting the venom in the countess's voice.

Salvatore had gone to Nicolette's room to escort her down to dinner, only to find she'd left without him. Perhaps Darian had escorted her down? No, Nic would have made mention to him first—unless Darian had caught her unaware.

Stepping out on the veranda, he passed by Darian, who managed a nod. Nicolette stood looking out over the gardens, her shoulders straight, hands behind her back. He could tell by body language alone that she was deep in thought, which made him wonder what had happened in the time he had left his room until now.

"Hello, Salvatore."

"How did you know it was me?" he asked, kissing her cheek. She smelled of lilacs, and looked stunning in a gorgeous creation of pink tulle over white silk that they had picked up in Paris. How innocent she looked with her auburn hair pulled up high, pearls weaved through the silky strands, and her green eyes and pink lips accented by a light touch of rouge.

"I know the sound of your footsteps."

"Very impressive."

She laughed lightly. "I'm glad you think so."

"So, how are you this evening?"

"I am well." Her voice lacked conviction.

"Liar."

She looked at him under dark lashes. "You know me better than I know myself."

He searched her face, noting the obvious. Her color was high, her lips red, swollen. She trembled as well. "What did he do?" he asked, not sure he wanted to hear the answer.

She shook her head. "Nothing."

He took her hand and led her down another path, away from the lights. "Come, tell me what happened."

Her fingers tightened within his own. "He wants me."

He waited for the exhilaration to come, but it didn't. Instead, he felt sick to his stomach. "Did he say as much?"

She shook her head. "No, but I can see it in his eyes…in his manner. He looks at me as though I am naked, and he wanted me to touch him intimately."

The words hit Salvatore with a force he did not expect. He would kill the bastard!

Her eyes narrowed. "I understand your hatred toward Darian, but are we right to come between him and Elizabeth? What will come of it in the end? What if ruining this marriage means we'll be ruining our career? We have worked too hard to get where we are now."

He watched her for a few seconds, gauging her words. All it would take would be a single word from him and it would be over—yet, his need for revenge was so strong, it controlled his every thought. He had the ability to ruin the Kedgwick dynasty, and it was within his grasp. This revenge was something he had yearned for from the day his father had tossed his mother and him out on their ears. Still he remembered his father's hated words—*Whore, take that son of a bitch away from here. I never want to set eyes on that dark-skinned bastard again.*

Salvatore shook away the memory. What if Nic was right? What if getting the revenge he craved cost them their career? *And what if Darian falls in love with Nicolette?* His conscience goaded him. His throat tightened at the prospect. "I can tell the countess you are unwell. We can leave for London posthaste."

She stopped in midstep, turned and looked him straight in the eye. "There is nothing I will not do for you. You know that?"

He nodded. "Of course."

Her gaze searched his. "I need to ask a favor."

His heart pounded. "Anything."

She looked down at her feet, took a deep breath and then met his gaze again. "Kiss me."

He blinked, unsure he had heard her correctly. "Sorry?"

"Darian kissed me tonight, and had it not been for his mother's interruption, it would have gone further. I know for certain he will try again when next we meet. I have never kissed like...lovers do, and I don't want to be shocked again."

Salvatore's first response was to flat-out deny her. However, he knew that if he said no, she was just reckless enough to find someone who would, and that would not do.

With his mind made up, he leaned forward and lightly kissed her on the lips. "There." He took a quick step back.

She blinked rapidly and her mouth dropped. "That's it?" She was clearly disappointed.

He frowned, his masculine pride injured. "I kissed you."

"I meant a *real* kiss. Like men and women kiss when they are in love." She took the step that separated them, looped her arms around his neck, lifted her chin and closed her eyes. "Now, do it right."

Salvatore's heart skipped a beat as he looked down at her upturned face. Gone was the young sprite in boys' clothes and pigtails. In her place was a woman full-grown, in the very flower of her youth…a beautiful woman who stirred the heart of every man that crossed her path.

His own heart trip-hammering, he leaned down and kissed her softly—once, twice, then slowly swept his tongue against the seam of her full lips. He heard her slight intake of breath and steadied himself for her to push away.

But she did not push away. Instead, she leaned into him, pressing her full breasts against his chest, and parting her lips to let him in.

His arms wrapped around her waist, pulling her tight against him as his tongue swept into the sweet recesses of her mouth. A moan escaped her as her tongue danced with his, and for a moment he lost all track of time and place. It was just the two of them, in the garden, with the sound of the fountain in the background.

With every stroke of her tongue against his own, he felt himself being drawn into her web. It had been ages since he had been with a woman, and his body responded in kind. He heard another moan, and realized too late that it had come from him.

His blood warmed his veins, coursing through his body, surging toward his groin, causing a deep ache within his now-throbbing manhood. Her hand slipped down his arm, her fingers grazing his forearm, then she pressed her hand flat against his stomach. The breath lodged in his throat. She was not doing what he thought she was doing, was she?

Her hand slipped past the waistband of his pants, her fingers grazing his cock head.

He nearly choked on his intake of breath.

"Salvatore! Nicolette!"

Hearing their names bellowed from nearby, Salvatore abruptly put her at arm's length. Nicolette stared up at him with mouth open, her lips swollen and red, and her eyes…were different. There was passion in those green depths that scared him even more than the erratic pounding of his heart. And even worse, her fingers were a fraction from his…

Dear God, what had he done?

"We will be right there," he said, his voice coming out lower than usual. He cleared his throat and removed her roving hand from his pants. "I trust that was adequate?"

Nicolette's lips curved the slightest bit and she nodded.

Taking her by the hand, he led her along the path at a brisk pace. It was a relief to see Mrs. Stromme, an outspoken American heiress in her late fifties, standing on the veranda, looking out over the gardens. She puffed on a cigar, her back toward the two of them. The fun-loving woman had told him last night that her husband forbade her to smoke. No wonder she looked ready to bolt.

Seeing a way out of the awkward tension, Salvatore put a finger to his lips, signaling silence. Nicolette nodded.

"Mrs. Stromme!"

The woman stifled a scream and dropped the cigar. "Salvatore! For the love of God, you nearly scared me out of my skin." She put her hand to her heart while grinding the cigar under her heel. "Come, you're late for dinner." She looked from Salvatore to Nicolette. "Dear, are you all right? You look a bit flushed."

Mrs. Stromme was right. Nicolette's cheeks were a flattering shade of pink, her eyes bright.

Nicolette glanced at Salvatore for a second and smiled innocently. "I'm quite well, thank you."

"When we heard your call, we practically ran the whole way," Salvatore said, extending his free arm for Mrs. Stromme. "Shall we?"

When they entered the dining room, all guests were seated. Salvatore helped Mrs. Stromme to her chair, then ushered Nicolette into her seat before taking his place at the opposite end of the table.

"Sorry for the delay," Salvatore said to the group who had gone silent at their entrance. "Nic and I are so accustomed to being seated last, that we often forget we hold up dinner in the process."

Understanding what it was to be last on the peerage list, and therefore the last to be seated, Mr. and Mrs. Stromme laughed aloud, breaking the uncomfortable silence.

Conversation resumed.

Salvatore glanced down the table from time to time to see how Nicolette fared. Sitting across from Darian, and beside a certain viscount who had finagled a place next to her, she held her own, smiling, laughing and charming all around her.

"Will you be playing tonight?" a woman asked, reminding Salvatore he had dinner companions to entertain; a newly married young lady, no older than Nicolette but far less attractive, and Charlotte. Elizabeth sat directly across from him and she smiled innocently at him over her wineglass.

"Yes, I will, Lady Mariweather," he replied.

Charlotte squeezed his thigh, and he nearly toppled the glass he had reached for. At any other time he might be tempted to flirt with the widow, but now was not the time. All his attention was focused on Nicolette and the kiss they had just shared. What had it meant…and why had he responded so passionately to her touch?

He looked down the table at Darian, who in turn watched Nicolette, much like a tiger ready to pounce on its prey. The man's attraction to her was obvious to everyone at the table, including Elizabeth who began chewing on her bottom lip in a very unattractive way. Darian's mother scowled at her son.

However, Darian seemed not to notice anyone except Nicolette.

Salvatore lifted the glass to his lips and swallowed the too-dry wine. He winced. The Kedgwick fortune *must* be in danger.

Nicolette laughed aloud, bringing Salvatore's attention back to that end of the table. She appeared so happy, her cheeks still pink, her smile wide, dimples exposed, eyes bright and alive as she leaned toward the viscount and whispered something in his ear.

"You are ever watchful of your partner," Charlotte said, one side of her mouth lifting in a coy smirk.

"I apologize. I do not mean to be inattentive to you beauties, but Nic was not feeling well earlier. That was one of the reasons we were late. I was considering bowing out for the night."

Charlotte frowned. "But you are to play this evening."

Salvatore nodded. "All women must think alike, for that is exactly what Nic said. She told me that we must earn our pay."

"I can think of more enjoyable ways to earn your pay," Lady Mariweather murmured close to his ear, her hot look telling him that he had not misread the invitation in her voice.

Sadly enough there had been a time in his life when he had been tempted to sell his body to the wealthy women of *the ton*. He had drawn the interest of women from all walks of life, those from the brothel he'd grown up in were no exception. He knew boys from the streets who made their living that way. But he always had Nicolette to consider, and she had never strayed from his side, making that lifestyle impossible. Thank God.

Throughout the various courses he looked up to find Nicolette watching Darian, her gaze lingering before glancing at Salvatore. He smiled reassuringly, then pushed food around his plate, as he had no appetite, all the while keeping up on the lackluster conversation going on about him, and fending off the advances of the widow who grew more aggressive, her hand inching up his thigh with each course.

It was with vast relief the countess stood and announced the women would be adjourning to the drawing room to take tea, while the men had cigars and a glass of port.

Rather than having a drink with the men, Salvatore immediately sought out Nicolette, who was already seated at the piano. "Ready?"

"I thought dinner would never end," she said, brushing a wayward curl from her face, only to have it bounce right back.

With a knowing smile, he smoothed the lock over her ear, trying without success to forget the kiss they had shared. How lovely she was. No wonder men flocked to her. "The wine was horrible, wasn't it?"

"Indeed, it was horrible."

He laughed under his breath, amazed how they thought so much alike.

Too soon the guests entered. Salvatore reached for his violin. He noticed Darian once again made his way to the very back of the room. Obviously he wanted to look his fill at Nicolette while mama and betrothed weren't breathing down his neck.

Once everyone was seated, Salvatore nodded at Nic. She smiled and closed her eyes, her long lashes resting against high cheekbones. His stomach tightened, for she looked just as she had when he'd kissed her earlier in the garden.

Pulling his attention from her to the music, he tried to forget the feel of her lips on his, the sound of her sighs, the feel of her full breasts smashed against his chest…the brush of her fingers against his cock…

What in the hell was the matter with him?

Try as he might to forget the moment, the image haunted him. Though he played song after song without fault, he felt a pang of guilt. He had never been so distracted.

Forcing himself to concentrate on the audience, he noted the women watching him—while all the men, save for the effeminate footman making cow eyes at him, watched Nicolette.

A servant handed Darian a glass of Madeira and nodded toward Nicolette. Salvatore could read his lips, "From the lady at the piano."

Salvatore glanced over at Nicolette to find her watching Darian. Darian lifted the glass in mock salute and Nic's lips curved into a soft, promising smile.

His stomach churned.

She was fast learning the game of seduction.

Nic's gaze caught Salvatore's. She didn't even blink as her fingers pounded on the keys, then softly gave way to a sweet melodious tune that had haunted him since the first time she had played it for him. Her song…and she was playing it for Darian. The knowledge cut to the quick and he looked away before she could read the disappointment in his eyes.

The score was filled with crescendos so intense that even the hair on Salvatore's arms stood on end and his throat tightened. Focusing, he put everything he was into the thundering climax that came right before an abrupt stop. For a moment there was silence, then the crowd jumped to their feet. Even Darian set the now-empty glass down, and joined in the applause.

Salvatore released an unsteady breath. They had never played with such energy, and the crowd loved it. Putting bow and violin beneath one arm, and taking Nicolette's hand with the other, he bowed and she curtsied.

"I am going to him," she said, and before he could get a word in, she was off, heading toward the back of the room where Darian watched her approach with a devil-may-care smile.

If possible, at that moment Salvatore hated his brother even more.

* * * * *

Nicolette's heart hammered as she approached Darian. If Salvatore wanted her to seduce Darian, then seduce him she would.

No more nervousness, no more qualms.

If only she could stop thinking about the kiss with Salvatore in the garden. The way his lips had tasted, and how wonderful it had been in comparison to Darian's kiss on the veranda.

She stopped before Darian, who reached out, grabbed her trembling hand and brought it to his lips.

She forced a smile. "Did you enjoy the Madeira?"

"Indeed, I did."

"I hope it will help you sleep this evening."

A dark brow lifted. "I'm sure I will sleep fine. Thank you."

The look in his eyes was predatory, and as his gaze slipped down her body, she shifted on her feet. She was in way over her head. "What did you think of the song?"

He leaned forward, his lips grazing her ear. "It was amazing, just as you are amazing."

His breath against her neck was hot. His nearness almost suffocating. She resisted the urge to step back and instead replied, "I am glad you enjoyed it."

"I want what you are offering, Nicolette."

His bluntness took her unaware. She opened her mouth but could not form any words.

"Come to me tonight. My room is on the second floor, west wing, third door on your right, which you will find unlocked." He nodded at a gentleman that passed by them before leaning closer. "I must ask for complete discretion."

Her heart pounded loud in her ears. "Tonight? I am quite tired."

He grinned, though it didn't quite reach his eyes. "You can sleep tomorrow. My servants are discreet. I will see to it that you are undisturbed so that you can rest."

The way he said it implied that he would keep her up all night. She abruptly shifted her gaze to his right and was relieved to find Elizabeth coming their way.

Nicolette smiled wide...and received a cool frown from the other woman, who had every right to be furious with her. Nicolette had felt more than a little guilty from the first time they'd met. After all, everyone in the room had to have seen the way Darian watched her throughout dinner, the way his eyes had slipped to her breasts, the heat there.

The countess had glared throughout dinner, reminding Nicolette about the horrid kiss she'd witnessed. Even the viscount had whispered under his breath that the earl was in rare form.

"Good evening, Lady Elizabeth," Nicolette said with as much joviality as she could muster.

Thankfully Darian released Nicolette's hand.

Darian smiled down at Elizabeth like the caring fiancé he should be, but was far from. Elizabeth in turn wrapped her hand in the crook of his arm, the gesture possessive. "Dearest, I was just telling Miss Rockwell how wonderfully she played."

Elizabeth looked up at Darian and genuinely smiled, relief evident on her face at her fiancé's warm welcome. "You both played amazing."

"Well, thank you," Salvatore said, stepping from behind Elizabeth to take Nicolette's hand. He kissed it softly. "I apologize for my absence, my sweet. I promised Lord Dancher I would have a brandy with him, but apparently the brandy got to him before I could, for he has already retired."

Nicolette's heart skittered, from both relief and excitement. He had not abandoned her after all.

Elizabeth laughed, watching Salvatore intently. A slight blush tinged her cheeks, and her eyes sparkled. Salvatore had already cast his spell over Darian's fiancée, it seemed. In fact, it appeared every woman present had been smitten by his charm.

"I am glad you enjoyed the performance," Nicolette said, squeezing Salvatore's hand. "I apologize for retiring so early, but it has been a long day and I fear I am in need of rest."

"Indeed," Salvatore injected. "I wish to retire as well, so we will bid you goodnight."

Even as she walked away, hand in hand with Salvatore, she could still feel Darian's eyes on her. He had made it clear with not only his words, but his smoldering stare just now, that he wanted her tonight, and he wasn't going to take no for an answer.

Chapter Four

ഌ

Salvatore woke early from a near restless night of sleep. The sensual dreams of the night before left him agitated and confused.

Nicolette had come to him in his dreams, kissing him, laying beside him, touching him, as one would a lover. He had taken her beneath him, entered her sweet body and she had cried out his name, meeting him thrust for thrust. He had awoken drenched in sweat, his heart pounding, his cock throbbing.

He needed to find a cold lake to jump into.

Dressing, Salvatore walked across the hall to Nicolette's room and knocked. When no answer came, he stepped in and found the room empty.

Last night he had been surprised by her desire to leave the party so early. Before Elizabeth had appeared at Darian's side, Nicolette and the earl had been standing at the back of the room, talking intimately…like lovers awaiting a tryst.

He took a steadying breath.

Be careful what you wish for. How many times had his mother warned him of that very thing? She'd been right, because now he wondered what in the world had possessed him to have Nicolette seduce a man that could easily break her heart.

Glancing at her empty bed, memories of the erotic dream came back to him, taunting him.

He forced himself to focus on where she might be, instead of the things they had done in his dream.

Nicolette was accustomed to late nights, so she rarely woke before ten o'clock. Unless… He shook his head. No, she would not have spent the night with Darian.

Or would she?

Her words came back to haunt him. *There's nothing I would not do for you.* With a calm he didn't feel, he left her bedchamber and went straight for the dining room, where a few guests were eating heartily from the food piled on sideboards that threatened collapse beneath the veritable feast.

Seeing that Nicolette was not amongst the diners, he walked back down the hall, out onto the veranda, thinking she might be taking a turn about the gardens. Having checked every drawing room and the library, he finally headed for Darian's study.

The door was shut, and it was all he could do not to press his ear against it to hear. Thankfully he refrained from doing so, for the butler appeared out of nowhere. "May I help you, sir?"

"No, thank you." Salvatore knocked on the study door.

"Enter."

Salvatore rolled his eyes at the command, and entered the dark-paneled room to find Darian at his desk and his mother in a nearby chair. "Good morning, Lady Kedgwick. Lord Kedgwick, have you seen Nicolette this morning?"

Darian looked surprised by the question. "No…perhaps she is sleeping."

"I have already been to her room. She is not there."

"Perhaps she spent the night with someone," the countess said, the words harsh and clipped.

Salvatore shook his head and forced civility. "Nicolette slept in her own room last night. I have been searching for over an hour. I thought perhaps you would know where she was."

"Why would my son know of her whereabouts?" the countess asked, looking from Salvatore to Darian, who appeared irritated by her question.

"Why indeed," Salvatore said, before backing out of the room. "Sorry to have disturbed you."

Concerned, Salvatore raced toward the stables. A young boy jumped at the sight of him. "Sir, may I be of assistance?"

"I am searching for a young lady. She stands about your height, with auburn hair and — "

"She left two hours ago." The boy shifted on his feet. "I told her I thought she should not go out alone, especially when there's a storm on the way."

Relieved, yet furious Nic had been so reckless, Salvatore mounted and rode like the devil was at his heels.

For miles he rode, seeing nothing but vast land before him. The cool air soon gave way to sprinkles before turning into pounding rain. With every minute that passed, his concern grew to the point different scenarios raced through his mind. What if Nicolette had been thrown from the horse? Or worse? One horrifying image after another played itself over in his head.

A loud crack of thunder sounded just as he came upon an old cottage weathered by time. He heard the whinny of a horse, and seeing a gray mare, knew that he had found Nicolette.

Relaxing now that he'd found her, Salvatore dismounted and told himself to let go of his anger and just be thankful she was all right. She was not his daughter, nor his sibling. He must stop treating her as he would one under his care. She was a grown woman who could make her own decisions, and mistakes…or maybe this time it was *his* mistake.

Tethering his horse to a nearby tree, he made his way to the cottage, where old lace curtains, yellowed from time, hung askew on the windows. He knocked softly, and Nicolette immediately opened the door. She was soaked to the skin, her hair plastered to her head, emphasizing her delicate bone structure.

"Salvatore," she said, surprise evident in her voice as she hugged him tight. "You are positively soaked to the skin."

"I am not the only one," he said, putting her at arm's length. "Do you realize how foolish you were to ride away from the manor? You could have told me where you were going. I was scared senseless."

She pulled him inside the small cottage that's warmth enveloped him. Already she had set a fire in the small stove, and had a pot of water boiling. "Salvatore, you worry too much. I am a woman, not a child. You were the one who taught me to embrace my independence. True, I lost my way in the rain, but as luck would have it, I came upon this cottage…and all is well."

Salvatore took off his coat and flung it over one of the three chairs in the room. "You shall catch your death if you don't take those clothes off," he said, turning toward the stove, reaching out to its warmth.

"Now that you are here to protect me, I shall do just that." He caught the sarcasm in her voice, taunting him. He did not dare look at her, just in case she had started to undress.

Staring at the pot of boiling water, he told himself that he would be able to watch her take Darian as a lover. After all, he had been the one to come up with the plan for her to seduce him. An image of Nic in his brother's bed made the blood boil in his veins, just like the water that boiled over on the stove.

Nicolette reached out, her petticoat wrapped around her hand, to take the pot from the stove. She stood with just her chemise on, the material transparent. He swallowed hard.

"Here, put these over that chair." She tossed him her riding habit and petticoats. With heart pounding loud in his ears, he placed the wet garments over the nearby chair, trying his hardest to keep his gaze averted from her near-naked body.

Trembling, he stripped off his shirt and held it out to her, keeping his gaze focused solely on her face. "Put this on." To his dismay, his voice came out huskier than intended.

In all their years together he had not seen her naked—until now. He could not help but dare a glance down her body, which was still covered by the wet chemise. His stomach tightened. She was perfection, from the rosy tips of her full breasts, to the triangle of auburn curls that covered her sex.

"Just a second." Without warning she pulled the chemise from her body and tossed it over his shoulder, before taking the shirt from him. Goose pimples covered her body, her nipples tightening further. It was all he could do not to crush her in his embrace, to give her comfort...and so much more.

"I'm sorry you had to come after me."

He turned away and ran a trembling hand down his face.

"But then again, you were probably ready to get out of that stifling house. I do not know how we will be able to bear it for an entire week."

Nicolette walked up to him. His shirt was much too large on her small frame, falling to mid-thigh, leaving her long legs bare to his gaze. He swallowed hard and looked away. "I was worried about you."

With a heavy sigh, she put her arm through his and lay her head on his shoulder. "What would I do without you, Salvatore?"

The blood roared in his ears. What was happening to him? Yesterday they had kissed and everything had changed. It was as though he had become aware of the beauty at his side for the first time. "And I without you," he whispered, the thought of losing her unbearable.

Nicolette sat down on one of the chairs. Dear lord her legs were long. How come he had not noticed before?

"I could spend the whole day here with you." Her words were soft...as was her expression. "Sometimes I get so tired of working, of always having to be on my best behavior. Wouldn't it be nice to have a place to call home? A place where we could just lay around in front of the fire, listen to the storm outside—just as we are now?"

It was as though he were seeing her for the first time. And as she stretched her arms overhead, bringing the shirt even higher, blood filled his groin, causing an unfamiliar ache deep inside him.

He turned away, toward the window, where he pulled back the old curtain and looked out at the rain that was blowing sideways. The wind howled, sending a cold gust of air through the cracks in the window. When would the storm break? If they spent the entire afternoon alone here, speculation would run rampant.

Why should he care what anyone thought? He never had before.

"Salvatore?"

"Hmmmm?" He turned to find her watching him. Her gaze roamed the length of his body and up again, like a woman studying her lover. His mouth went dry. "You have a beautiful body, Salvatore. Do you realize I have not seen you without a shirt since you were a child?" She flashed a coy smile.

"You most certainly are not a boy. You are so broad of shoulder, and your chest is strong and wide, and yet your waist is narrow. When you move I can see the muscle shift beneath your olive skin. Truly, you are as beautiful as Michelangelo's David."

Salvatore released his breath in a rush. She had no idea what her soft words were doing to him—what they would do to any man.

Her expression changed abruptly. "Salvatore, I must be honest with you. Darian wants to meet me. He told me that he wanted what I offered. He told me to come to his room, that he would leave it unlocked. He told me that his servants are discreet."

Salvatore pulled up a chair and sat forward. "What else did he say?"

"He stopped by my room last night. He knocked on the door, but I feigned sleep. It was early in the morning when I woke and found a letter had been slipped beneath my door." She reached toward her wet dress, fished in the pocket and pulled out a letter. "I was restless, so I went for a ride, hoping that I would find the courage to face him."

"May I see it?"

She handed it to him.

Salvatore swallowed hard, his emotions in turmoil as he unfolded the damp letter. The ink had smeared from the rain, but the words were legible.

I need to see you.

Come to me, please.

Yours, D.

The words hit Salvatore like a fist to his gut. Darian wanted her. In that, they had succeeded. But where would it end? Would he fall in love with her, call off his wedding to Elizabeth, and despite the fact of losing all the riches, still live happily ever after with Nicolette as his wife? "No!"

He didn't realize he'd said the word aloud until Nicolette replied, "No?"

Unable to sit still, Salvatore paced. "Do not meet him in his room."

She looked stricken. "I...I did not. That is why I left. I needed time to collect my thoughts."

He stopped before her. "Why did you not come to me? We could have talked about this." His voice came out harsher than intended.

She hesitated, then looked away, toward the fire, casting her profile in soft light. "Because I thought you would tell me to go to him…and I could not bring myself to do that."

He closed his eyes for a brief moment, feeling like a cad. Lifting her chin with his hand, he urged her to meet his gaze. "I would never do that to you. I've told you before that if you desire to leave, we can do that."

She reached up and took hold of his hand. "Salvatore, I want you to show me how to please a man in every way."

Nicolette waited for Salvatore's response. His mouth opened but no words came. Her stomach clenched. It was as she thought—he felt nothing for her other than a brotherly-like concern.

She dropped his hand. "I didn't mean to embarrass you."

He shook his head. "I'm not embarrassed. I just did not anticipate such a question."

"I know he believes we are lovers. What do I do when he expects me to know how to make love, and instead I know nothing of how it is done? I have no experience with men, and who better to teach me than the man I love most?"

His throat convulsed when he swallowed. "What is it you want me to show you exactly?"

Her gaze lingered on his handsome features—the jutting cheekbones, the strong jaw, the full gorgeous lips. She took the step that separated them and wrapped her arms around his neck. "Show me where I should place my hands when he kisses me. Tell me what feels good to a man."

It felt wonderful to touch him, to feel his skin rubbing against hers. How she wanted to take off the shirt and experience what it would feel like to have nothing, not even fabric, between them.

His arms slid around her waist. "Let's start with a kiss then." The words hadn't left his mouth when his lips descended on hers. The kiss started soft, as light as a butterfly's wings.

Nicolette could feel the beating of Salvatore's heart against her own. It pounded hard, and she wondered if he was as excited as she was. She parted her lips, inviting him to enter, and he did not disappoint. His tongue stroked hers, urging her to play along.

And she did. His arms tightened around her, making her feel safe and secure. She shifted slightly, allowing one of her arms to creep under his, giving her access to his back. The hard muscles bunched beneath her questing fingers, the skin smooth and soft to the touch. She traced an invisible line along his spine with her fingers, brushing along the waistband of his pants.

He deepened the kiss, his hand coming up to anchor her head, his fingers weaving through her hair.

Her blood thickened in her veins, and a warmth swooped low down into her stomach and between her legs.

Her hand roamed lower, over his tight buttock, and she felt his intake of breath. He didn't stop though. He kept right on kissing her.

"Touch me," she whispered against his lips.

His long-fingered hands encompassed her waist, resting on her hips, then moved lower, over her buttocks, pulling her against him. Feeling the hard ridge of his manhood pressed against the juncture of her thighs, Nicolette's heart gave a steady jolt. One hand moved up, along her back, in a soothing gesture.

Every inch of her body felt on fire. Her nipples thrust against his chest, and she yearned for him to touch her there, yet she could not bring herself to utter the words.

As though he could read her mind, his lips left hers, kissing her along her jaw, her ear, his tongue sliding along the sensitive curve. Nicolette inhaled, taking in his masculine scent as his mouth moved along her neck, and then her collarbone.

Her hands wove through his hair, the feel of his lips on her flesh making her yearn for more than he would be willing to give. If only he loved her the way she loved him…

He pulled the shirt up and over her head, tossing it aside. His gold eyes had darkened. She had never seen him look that way. So sensual, so passionate, and her heart soared knowing *she* had caused such a reaction.

The thought was forgotten as he lowered his head and took a nipple into his mouth. The breath caught in Nicolette's throat as his tongue laved her, circling the sensitive peak, then sucking, using his teeth just the slightest bit to make her stomach flip. Her head fell back on her shoulders, enjoying the new sensations.

A deep ache pulsed within her, between her legs. Apparently she was not so different than her mother, who had made her living pleasuring men, and being pleasured in return.

Salvatore's mouth left her breast, and moved to the other. His hand encompassed the other breast, and he rolled her nipple between thumb and forefinger.

She looked down at him. His eyes were closed, the long lashes fanning against his high cheekbones. As though sensing her stare, he opened his eyes and smiled against her breast, his tongue snaking out, licking her nipple.

"Salvatore, I want…" She couldn't find the words.

He didn't stop. He continued pleasuring her, his mouth taking her ever higher to a pinnacle she wanted to reach, to experience. His other hand moved down, over her quivering stomach, to her woman's mound. His fingers stroked the slick folds, running along the seam, flicking against a part of her she had not known existed. It seemed he knew her body better than she did. He kissed her, his fingers working their magic, the pad of his thumb resting on the hidden nub, while he slipped a finger inside her.

Her body clutched him, and as he moved the finger in and out of her, her body tightened, and every nerve in her body tensed. Salvatore's kiss deepened, and he added another finger. Nicolette arched against his hand, her breath catching in her throat as she soared to the stars, her body feeling like it had been launched to the heavens.

As her breathing returned to normal, she opened her eyes and Salvatore smiled. His finger slipped from her, and he hugged her tight. She rested her head on his shoulder, trying to catch her breath.

Dear god, she had experienced just a tiny part of lovemaking…and she wanted so much more.

Salvatore held Nicolette tightly. She trembled in his arms, and still her heart pounded as loudly as his own.

He should be shot. What had possessed him to take the *lesson* to such a level? He had thought to merely kiss her, to teach her just a little of what happened between a man and a woman, but his desire had escalated from teaching to white-hot need. Her soft moans had told him she enjoyed what he was doing, and once she had touched him so intimately, he had not been able to hold back.

Nicolette's body would be imprinted on his mind for all eternity. Her full breasts with the rose-pink colored nipples had set his blood on fire. The patch of thick curls that covered her sex, hiding the treasure within, had beckoned him, and he had been unable to keep from touching her…from sliding his fingers within her. She had been so unbelievably tight there, so hot, and her orgasm had come quickly, with an intensity that left them both shaking.

She kissed his bare shoulder, then his collarbone. It seemed she wanted more. Already his cock strained against his pants. She must feel what she did to him. She had to. Sweat beaded his brow as her lips made a trail up his neck, along his jaw. Dear lord, she must stop now, or he would not be able to.

His heart thundered. He put her at arm's length. That wasn't his heart he heard—it was horse's hooves, and they were headed this way.

"Someone is coming," he said, grabbing her chemise and handing it to her. "Put your clothes on."

With lightning speed, Salvatore slipped on his shirt, then helped Nicolette into her dress. He had just finished buttoning her gown when through the curtains he saw someone approach.

Darian.

Nicolette made herself busy by making tea, and Salvatore opened the door. "Darian, what a surprise."

Darian stepped past Salvatore into the cabin. Seeing Nicolette, he smiled, clearly relieved. "So, you did find her. When you did not return right away, I became worried and thought I would search for her myself."

Nicolette smiled softly at Darian. "I am flattered that you left your guests to search for me."

"You are most important to me, Nicolette. I think you know that."

Salvatore clenched his teeth and refrained from commenting. He looked at Nicolette, who watched Darian with a sweet expression. Her cheeks were still flushed from their lovemaking, her hair falling down around her in thick waves, making her look so innocent and vulnerable.

She sensed his gaze, but she did not let on. Darian leaned into her and whispered something in her ear. Her brows lifted slightly and she grinned.

He should leave, allow the seduction to begin, especially now that Nicolette knew more than she had this morning in how to please a man. His body had responded to her questing hands and lips on his body.

"The rain is about to break," Darian said, taking the cup of tea Nicolette offered. "We should be able to return to the manor before too long."

Thank God!

Salvatore suddenly felt a great desire to be as far away from the cabin and Darian Tremayne as he could get.

"You were remiss in leaving the manor, Nicolette. You should have told someone where you were going. You had everyone quite concerned, especially your partner." Darian glanced at Salvatore. "Isn't that right?"

Salvatore nodded.

"I knew he would be, but I could not prevent the storm that came," Nicolette replied, before taking a sip of tea.

"Perhaps you should take the weather into consideration before you ride next time. You took an unjustifiable risk."

Nicolette turned back to Darian, her brows furrowed. "Is it so horrible to test oneself...to see where it will lead you? Honestly, what is so bad about taking a risk?"

Salvatore frowned. What was she talking about? Obviously something more than just taking a ride during a storm.

"Most risks are foolhardy, yet some are worth taking," Darian replied, his voice lower, seductive.

Nicolette's lips quirked. "What would you know of risks, aside from being caught in a married woman's bed?"

Salvatore hid a smile. Darian looked at Nicolette, his expression indecipherable. "Touché," he said, reaching out to take hold of Nicolette's hand, bringing it to his lips. "Is that jealousy I hear in your voice?"

Oh for the love of God!

Nicolette smiled prettily. "Perhaps."

"I'm flattered."

Salvatore didn't know whom he wished to strangle more at that moment.

"Now tell me, Nicolette, do you always take chances?" Darian all but purred.

"Always," she replied without hesitation, and Salvatore had to refrain from cursing, especially when Darian's thumb brushed back and forth over Nicolette's hand.

Salvatore opened the door and the sun poured in. "Look, the storm has passed. We should be getting on our way." Without another word, he stepped outside.

Chapter Five

ಬ

"How many lovers have you had, Nicolette?" Darian asked, a dark brow lifted in question.

"How many have you had?"

He smiled. "I asked you first."

She stared at him, wondering why it was women flocked to him in droves. It had to be the money and the title, because he was the most conceited man on the planet. For the past ten minutes she had listened while he droned on about his crops in Virginia, and then the expensive ring he had purchased while in London the week before. Nicolette glanced at Salvatore who rode ahead of them, his shoulders ramrod straight. He stayed within hearing distance, she knew that much.

Her body still burned from where Salvatore had touched her earlier. If only Darian had not arrived, she would have experienced everything.

"I do not count my conquests."

Apparently that was not the answer he was looking for, because he frowned. "So, you have had many?"

She shrugged. "Does that bother you?"

"Perhaps." To make amends, he quickly added, "I did not mean to offend you."

She laughed under her breath. "Oh, yes you did. You would never speak to another woman in such a way, but I am not every other woman, now am I?"

"No, you are not like any other woman I have met." He looked ahead to Salvatore, and brought his horse closer. "Why did you not come to me last night? I waited for you."

"I fell asleep."

"Liar."

She laughed. "There are eyes everywhere, Kedgwick. I know that you have to be most careful, especially since your betrothed is underfoot."

At the mention of Elizabeth, Darian rolled his eyes. "If only I did not have to marry that woman." He released a heavy sigh. "What I would give to marry you instead. How I would rush to the altar."

"You cannot marry me. I do not have blue enough blood."

His gaze shifted from hers, to her chest. "True, you can not be my wife, but you could be my mistress."

Feeling as though she'd been slapped, Nicolette lifted her chin. "I would never be a kept woman."

Disappointment flashed in his eyes. "I would give you anything you desired. A home, jewels, gowns. You would never have to play again."

"I would never stop playing, particularly for a man. Music is my life, my passion."

She could tell by the way he clenched his jaw, that he had not expected such a revelation. He seemed infuriated. "I want you, Nicolette, and I believe you want me as well. I do not want to argue with you, I want to love you."

He was too close. She could feel his breath against her face. The need in his voice made her increasingly uncomfortable. "I thought you were different, Kedgwick. But I can plainly see you are not." Without another word, she put her knees to the horse's sides and sped forward, past Salvatore.

Darian raced after and she could hear him catching up. A moment later he reached out, ripped the reins from her, and pulled her close. Before she could blink, his lips captured hers in a kiss that was not at all gentle, his teeth pressing hard against her upper lip.

Disgusted, Nicolette pulled away.

Darian's eyes were wild. "I did not mean to offend you."

She resisted the urge to slap him. "Yes, you did."

"This is not over between us...we *will* finish this," he said, his voice low and husky.

Thankfully she was saved from replying when Salvatore approached, reining in beside Nicolette.

"Did the horse throw a shoe?" Salvatore asked, his gaze searching her face. He looked...angry. Her heart gave a jolt. Was he jealous? His eyes locked on her lips, which were no doubt swollen from Darian's kiss.

She smiled inwardly. He *was* jealous!

"No, it was just a rock lodged in the hoof," Darian said before Nicolette could form a reply.

* * * * *

Salvatore remained silent during dinner. Sitting directly across from Nicolette, he made small talk with his dinner companions, Charlotte managing her usual place at his side. Nicolette wondered if she groped him beneath the table as she was known to do. The very thought made her blood boil.

Nicolette could not remember a time she had seen Salvatore with a woman. True, they did not spend a lot of time apart, but there were nights he would tell her he had errands to run and would not return until morning. Once she had been able to smell perfume on his shirt. He had told her it was from Madame la Monte, the madam of the brothel where their mothers worked and they had lived.

Having experienced just a taste of what making love would be like, Nicolette stared at her partner. She had always thought him more handsome than any man she'd known. So different from the conceited earl who sat three people down to her right, staring at her, no doubt hoping to catch her attention.

Darian's kiss had made her ill to her stomach. The complete opposite effect that Salvatore's kiss had had on her.

Memories of the precious moments in the cabin made her blood warm. The feel of Salvatore's mouth on her breasts, his tongue laving her nipples, the feel of his long fingers inside her, stroking her as though he knew her body better than she did. Her gaze shifted to his long-fingered hand, which rested on his glass. Hands that could play the violin, the piano and any instrument he chose. Hands that could play a woman, making her body sing.

She felt like a moth being lured to a flame. Here she was supposed to be seducing Darian for Salvatore, and instead she was hoping to seduce Salvatore. She could not help it. She had loved him for too long, and he had always looked at her and treated her like a child.

But she would no longer lie to herself. She wanted more. Salvatore would be her tutor, and she would not stop with the lessons. The only problem she could foresee was keeping Darian at bay.

She closed her eyes for a brief moment. Lord, but she was confused. Above all else she had to remember this was only a game. She must keep Darian at arm's length. Hopefully she could divert suspicion from the countess and Elizabeth. Apparently the duke himself would be showing up tomorrow morning, which meant it would be even harder for Darian to find time alone with her.

Thank goodness.

Salvatore jumped, and nearly knocked his glass over. Charlotte cast him a sheepish smile and he managed a tight grin.

No doubt her hand was latched onto Salvatore's thigh — or somewhere even more intimate.

Nicolette's stomach rolled. Why didn't the woman prey on someone else? Someone like Darian?

Kicking off her slipper, Nicolette extended her foot and rubbed it against Salvatore's.

Salvatore's brows furrowed into a frown. He picked up his glass and took a long swallow.

Nicolette trailed her toes up along his ankle.

Salvatore glanced at Charlotte, who had turned away to speak to Viscount Aubrey. He then glanced to his right, at Mrs. Stromme, and then quickly looked away. He took another drink and then his gaze lifted to hers.

Nicolette smiled and lifted a brow.

Surprise flitted over his features, and then with a smirk, he jerked his foot away.

Taking a drink from her wineglass, she watched him as he in turn watched her. She continued to drink, letting the liquor burn its way down her throat. She welcomed the fire. Perhaps it would quench the flame of desire within her.

His eyes narrowed as she drained the entire glass. It seemed the father in him had returned.

"You are thirsty this evening?" the viscount beside her asked.

Pulling her gaze from Salvatore, Nicolette nodded. "Indeed, it has been a long day."

The viscount motioned for the footman to replenish her drink. She smiled prettily and caught Darian's gaze. His eyes were dark, his expression imploring. They had not spoken since they returned to the manor, when all three of them retired straight to their rooms.

Darian motioned to the veranda, apparently wanting to meet her outside after dinner. The footman poured her a drink. Breaking eye contact with Darian, she thanked the footman, took a sip of the wine and caught Salvatore's stare.

She finished the wine, set the glass down and focused all her attention on the plate before her.

* * * * *

Nicolette ignored Salvatore the rest of the night.

Looking gorgeous in a forest green gown, and wearing long white gloves, she looked the epitome of a princess. Having drank another glass of wine, she licked her lips.

A stirring began in the pit of Salvatore's stomach, growing outward as he remembered vividly the feel of those full lips under his, the velvety softness of her tongue, and the way she pressed her curvaceous body against him. When she had moaned and shifted her hips against him, it had very nearly been his undoing. She had been so wet for him, her hot, tight channel pulsing, drawing his finger in deeper.

Dear god, how had he allowed this to happen? How could he have gone so far with her? Now they could never return to how they once were. He had ruined everything.

Perhaps once they left Kedgwick Manor, the two of them could forget all that had happened here.

Liar! He could no more forget the feel of her body against his, the taste of her lips, the feel of her soft womanly curls against his palm as he stroked her, than he could quit breathing.

Even now he wanted her with a ferocity that terrified him. He cursed under his breath. She would seduce Darian, lead him to ruin, then they would leave, perhaps visit Greece for an extended time. Nicolette loved it in his mother's homeland, safe above the ocean in their own little rented villa, going swimming...sightseeing.

Dinner ended, and Salvatore stared at his half-full plate. What was happening to him? He had all but lost his appetite of late. It must be staying in this old tomb of a home, a constant reminder of the father who despised him that made him so restless.

You must never forget what he did to us. His mother's words to him on her deathbed burned within him, making him put aside all his romantic notions in regard to Nicolette. By week's end they would leave this place and never look back.

Darian slipped out the back door, and Nicolette stayed with the viscount for a few minutes before making her way out the opposite door. The countess was busy speaking with Elizabeth and a group of women, who laughed gaily, completely oblivious to the liaison happening right beneath their noses.

Salvatore walked toward the door Nicolette had departed and stepped out onto the veranda. The wind had kicked up, and he welcomed the breeze. He caught sight of someone entering the labyrinth and he started to follow but then stopped. What was he doing? He had to allow what was going to happen, to happen. He had asked for this. He had all but told her what to do, and now he must give her space.

With heavy heart, he headed to his room, not stopping by the table where a group of men had joined to play cards. He had never felt part of the aristocracy, had always disdained the men who did nothing for a living, save stroll through life on their ancestors' money and titles passed on to them. They had nothing in common with a man who had grown up on the streets of London, who knew what it was to want so badly that it consumed you.

He took the steps two at time, not stopping when the widow called out his name.

* * * * *

Nicolette entered the labyrinth, her heart pounding loudly in her ears with every step that took her deeper into the maze. She had an uneasy feeling. No one had followed her, and the night grew colder by the second.

She was ready to turn back when a hand snaked out and grabbed her. She gasped, but it was cut short as Darian's mouth came down upon hers. Darian groaned low in his throat as he pulled her tight to him, his mouth slanting against hers, his teeth pressing hard into her upper lip.

She winced from the pain, once again comparing the kiss with the one she'd shared earlier with Salvatore.

"I must have you," Darian said, pulling up her gown with both hands.

Nicolette pushed at him, but he held her tight, his eyes dark, wild.

"You have teased me mercilessly for days now. Last night you said you were too tired, and today at the cabin, the way you looked at me said what you felt. I know that look. I know that desire."

The way she had looked at him? Was he mad?

She had not looked that way because of him, but rather what she'd experienced with Salvatore.

"We cannot do this, not here."

"Why not?"

"Because, it's too cold."

He flashed a cocky grin. "I'll keep you warm, I promise."

"Kedgwick," she said, keeping her voice low, seductive. "I expected more from you than a tumble in the labyrinth."

He released a heavy sigh. "You try my patience, Nicolette."

"What if Elizabeth came upon us."

He shrugged. "I am not married yet."

"Yes, but you may as well be."

"I don't want to talk about her."

She lifted a brow. "You may not, but I fear I must, for both our sakes. What would the duke say if he found out about us? You could lose everything."

Darian frowned. "How do you know?"

"Everyone knows."

Running a hand through his hair, he said, "I despise the fact that I must marry a woman I feel nothing for. I feel like a child, my every movement being watched." Hearing footsteps, Darian pulled away from her. "Someone comes."

Nicolette practically fainted with relief, so relieved was she.

"You had best go," Darian said, pushing her toward the pathway, not wanting to be discovered.

"What of you?"

"I will find my way back."

Relieved, Nicolette started back the way she had come, and nearly ran into Charlotte, who weaved a little. Nicolette had noted the widow drank heavily each night. Tonight was no exception. She hiccupped and stumbled a little. "Nicolette, what are you doing out here?"

"I wanted solitude. And what of yourself, Lady Mariweather?"

"Please, call me Charlotte," she said, wine sloshing over the glass, onto the beaded bodice of her gown. "I came out for more of the same. I can not bear to be in the company of all those women, all of them looking down their noses at me."

Her interest piqued, Nicolette asked, "What do you think of Elizabeth?"

"Bah," the woman said, a wicked grin on her face. "As ugly as a post, and a personality to match."

"Indeed."

Lady Mariweather hiccuped again. "What a waste, especially for a man like Kedgwick. He is so virile, so handsome."

"You have been intimate with him?" Nicolette asked.

Charlotte snorted. "Who hasn't?"

Nicolette leaned forward and whispered in Lady Mariweather's ear. "He is just beyond us, in the center of the labyrinth. He told me he awaits someone. Is that someone you, I wonder?"

It took Charlotte a moment to realize what Nicolette meant, but she knew the moment comprehension sunk in, for she smoothed a hand down the front of her skirts and handed Nicolette her wineglass. "Do you think he waits for me?"

"I've little doubt, but you must hurry. You know how his mother keeps track of him."

Charlotte licked her bottom lip. "Indeed, I do. Well, it will not take long. Tah."

And with that, Charlotte weaved her way through the maze. Nicolette followed behind—staying far enough away from the stone bench where Darian stood, that she would not be noticed.

His surprise upon seeing Charlotte was obvious. He lifted his brows, and she could not hear what they said to each other. For a few moments they chatted, and then Charlotte launched herself into his arms, kissing Darian.

At first Kedgwick appeared amused, but when Charlotte caressed the obvious bulge in his pants, his expression changed completely.

Charlotte lifted her skirts, exposing dark stockings held up by rosette garters. She turned her back on Darian, leaned over the bench, and braced her hands on the stone bench. Her bare bottom was high in the air, an open invitation if ever there was one.

Darian unbuttoned his pants, exposing his long, thick arousal. He said something that made Charlotte giggle, then he slid his length inside the widow with a groan. His head fell back on his shoulders, his jaw clenched tight.

Charlotte sighed loudly as Darian thrust into her again and again. Nicolette watched for a moment, unable to look away at the sight, at the pleasure in both their faces.

A strange stirring crept into Nicolette's stomach, and lower to the flesh between her thighs. With a final glance, she left the two.

Once safely behind the closed door of her bedchamber, she sat down on her bed and ran her hand down her face. If Charlotte had not come along, it could have been her in that labyrinth with Darian.

Perhaps she should just come right out with it and tell Salvatore how she felt.

She stood up, then sat right back down. How would he feel if he knew she had failed yet again? Secretly she hoped Darian kept his distance. Perhaps befriending Charlotte would make things easier for her. In fact, why could she not encourage Charlotte to continue her liaison with Darian at the party? She could help Charlotte, know their whereabouts, and then send the countess, or even the duke looking for the two. It would still mean Darian's downfall, and she could leave with her conscience intact.

* * * * *

Darian walked back to his quarters, his mind racing. He had but a taste of Nicolette and now he knew it would never be enough. Her passion was overwhelming and the attraction between them was so fierce, it was disconcerting.

Had he actually thought that one taste, one touch, would be enough? Damn, if Charlotte had not come upon them it would have been Nicolette he had fucked instead of the widow, a woman he had bedded before right under her husband's nose. True, his body was sated for the time being, but it was not Charlotte that he craved.

No, it was Nicolette.

How would he get through the next week with her underfoot?

He was so deep in thought, he nearly ran into his mother as he rounded the corner.

Her gaze shifted from his, down the hall, toward Nicolette's room where he was heading. "Where have you been? I've been looking all over for you," she said, one dark brow lifted in question.

Though she no more than whispered, there was a shrill-like quality to her voice that he had never heard before, and it made him uneasy.

"What can you be thinking, Darian? You are cuckolding your intended right beneath her nose—and at your own engagement party, no less. Nicolette is a musician for God's sake. The daughter of a trollop. Must I remind—"

"I've heard enough, Mother. You forget she is here by your invitation."

She lifted her chin. "They invited themselves. I received word from Salvatore a fortnight ago. He asked to come."

Darian frowned. Nicolette had given him the impression that his mother had sought the duo out.

"Come, Darian? She is a beautiful woman and she is attracted to you, that much is obvious. They could live very generously off your wealth if you were to become her lover. And think about this…they had a standing invitation to play at Brooks' for the entire month, which would have paid quite nicely. Yet, here they do not expect or require payment, but rather do it as a favor. A favor to whom, I ask you? And, there is no one here that they would call a close friend. In fact, they are virtual strangers to most all our guests. Think on it…it makes no sense whatsoever."

He didn't want to consider that her words might hold any truth, but as the minutes ticked by and he thought back over the last couple of days, he had to wonder if Nicolette's affection toward him was indeed orchestrated. What if she and that too-pretty partner of hers did have an ulterior motive? He shook away the thought. Nicolette desired him—that was not too hard to believe, given he had been chased by more than one entertainer in his life.

"Perhaps they should leave," she injected, steering him back toward the staircase.

"That won't be necessary," he replied, intent on finding out the truth for himself. He had no intention of telling the two to leave...at least not until he had Nicolette in his bed.

She nodded. "Good, then I expect you to abide by my wishes and play the gracious host and groom-to-be. I know marriage is not an easy thing to accept, but it will benefit you and future generations of Kedgwicks. It is a matter of family honor that you do this."

"There are many women out there who want you simply on the merits of your title. Elizabeth is not one of those women. She will be a good wife, and the least you can do is be a faithful husband. Remember that her father will stand for nothing else. It is not like you have not had time to take your fill of women." Without another word she smiled tightly, then turned toward her quarters.

As he watched his mother go, he pondered her words. True, he had had a lot of women in his time, but none that could compare with Nicolette. None had her fire, or her spirit—a quality he found very appealing. The emotions she evoked in him were altogether too intense, particularly to a man who was to be married.

Chapter Six

ॐ

Nicolette had just finished breakfast when Darian walked into the dining room. To her right, Charlotte sat up straighter, a knowing smile on her lips as she glanced at Kedgwick, who completely ignored her.

Darian took a seat at the head of the table, nodded toward a servant and waited until he'd been served before meeting her gaze. Nicolette smiled, then lifted the china cup to her lips.

"How are you this morning, Nicolette?" he asked, his voice low, his eyes coming to rest on the low bodice of her gown.

Nicolette could see Charlotte bristle beside her. The woman lifted her chin a fraction and arched her back, her ample bosom near spilling from the tight confines of her amazing yellow gown. Darian glanced at the other woman and nodded. "Lady Mariweather."

Charlotte smiled prettily and nodded in return, her look so smoldering even the footman blushed.

Salvatore walked in a moment later. Wearing navy breeches, a white shirt and Hessian boots that were splattered with mud, it was obvious where he'd been. His long hair had been tied back in a queue, but a lock had come loose from the ribbon and fell against his neck and shoulders in lush waves.

Nicolette swallowed hard. He had never looked so desirable.

He went straight to the sideboard where he grabbed a plate and picked out a slice of ham and a few pieces of fresh fruit before taking the seat directly across from her.

"You were riding?" she asked, wondering why he had not woken her. He knew she loved to ride just as much as he did.

He looked up from his plate and stared at her. "Indeed, I did go for a ride."

She pursed her lips as he pierced the ham with his fork and lifted it to his lips. Those soft, full lips that she yearned to feel against her own.

He was male perfection. Tall, dark, beautiful, and with a talent that made women weep.

A buxom servant poured Salvatore a cup of tea, brushing up against him as she did so. Beside Nicolette, Charlotte chuckled under her breath.

Nicolette gave her a sidelong glance and Charlotte lifted her brows. "He is gorgeous," she whispered, and Nicolette nodded in agreement, not at all liking the way the widow's eyes settled on Salvatore.

"Are you finished riding for the day?" Darian asked, breaking the uncomfortable silence.

Salvatore looked up, his gaze meeting his brother's. He shrugged. "I am growing restless, I fear."

Darian looked like he'd been struck. "Indeed? Well, I would hate to think I had not done my duty by you. Why do we not go for a ride this afternoon."

"That would be wonderful," Nicolette said, ignoring Salvatore's displeasure.

"I would love to," Salvatore replied, turning to Darian. "How about we invite your fiancée along. I have missed her company of late."

Charlotte cleared her throat. Nicolette pushed her plate back from her. "Would you like to join us, Lady Mariweather?"

The widow grinned. "I would *love* to. Thank you so much for asking!"

Pleased to have an ally, Nicolette pushed back her chair. "Since I'm finished eating, I'll go change."

Charlotte stood beside her. "And I shall join you."

Nicolette went straight to her room and promised she would meet Charlotte at the foot of the steps in quarter of an hour. She browsed the armoire and decided on a forest green riding habit. Within minutes she changed, pinned on the hat, and made for the stairs where Charlotte waited. The widow wore a somber black that hugged her generous curves, and her black hat, including a huge peacock feather, sat atop her blonde braided hair.

The woman was absolutely breathtaking, and for a moment Nicolette had the insane urge to head back up the stairs and change into something more alluring.

Spying her, Charlotte beamed. "Come, the men are already at the stables."

They departed the house, and made their way down the staircase that led down to the immaculate gardens. Charlotte pulled on her gloves and nodded toward Elizabeth. "Look at that chit. She does not know the first thing about horseflesh."

True enough, Elizabeth stood with arms rigid, back poker-straight, as Darian tried to help her mount the gray mare. The woman's face was positively white. Finally, with struggle, Elizabeth settled into the sidesaddle, looking like she would rather be anywhere else.

"How ridiculous it is that a man such as the earl should be saddled with a child like Elizabeth for a bride." Charlotte shook her head. "And to have a father-in-law as morally strict as the Duke of Durham to boot. One can almost feel sorry for him."

"Almost?"

Charlotte grinned devilishly. "In truth, he deserves it. He has broken more hearts in England than any other man. He tires of his mistresses too easily, disposing of them the moment they get too clingy."

"You were one of those women?"

Charlotte scoffed. "Lord no! I was a married woman, so I had no expectations whatsoever. Our affair was brief, but fun, and I am glad to have rekindled it here while at Kedgwick Hall. A last hurrah, have you, before the Earl of Kedgwick is put to pasture."

"So you believe he will be forced to remain faithful to Elizabeth?"

"Let's just say the duke has eyes everywhere, and he will do what he must to ensure his only heir is happy."

Just then Salvatore stepped out of the stables, leading a large black mare. Having been brought up poor and in London, riding had been an activity both she and Salvatore had yearned for from afar. It had been Count de Vassey, a sweet man who bred horses just outside of Paris, who had introduced the two to horse riding. Every day they had ridden, and under de Vassey's tutelage, had learned to ride with skill, as well as care for horses. When they had left his home, the count had given them mounts, which they kept at a stable near London.

"How do you keep your hands off of him, Nicolette?" Charlotte asked, staring at Salvatore in a way that made her uncomfortable and…jealous.

A lanky groom led a horse and she mounted without help. Charlotte, however, looked toward Salvatore for assistance. Nicolette watched with a practiced smile, noting how Charlotte's gloved hand clenched around Salvatore's biceps. Did the woman have no shame?

Salvatore seemed not to mind. In fact, he flashed a wolfish smile, and lit up under the woman's attention. Any man would want Charlotte. She was beautiful, voluptuous, and had a wild streak that most men must find enticing. Plus, as she stated to Nicolette earlier, she had no expectations when it came to taking lovers, and therefore men weren't intimidated by her. All they expected was mutual satisfaction.

Did Salvatore want Charlotte? He had told her he thought her groping beneath the dinner table was taxing, but was he only saying that to make her feel better? Or did he actually enjoy having the woman, who was a few years his senior, panting for him?

With a wild whoop Charlotte was off like a shot, and Salvatore right behind her. Not to be left out of the fun, Nicolette kicked her mount and raced across the green grass.

The wind caught her hair, ripping it from her ribbon. The tresses blinded her for a moment. Ahead of her Charlotte darted off to the left, around a large hedge.

Nicolette wondered if Salvatore would go for the wall. She knew the minute he had committed. He leaned down, low over the horse's mane and jumped, the stallion making the wall with inches to spare.

Nicolette glanced over her shoulder to see Kedgwick and Elizabeth but a speck on the horizon. Without another thought, she put knees to the horse's flanks and jumped.

Charlotte and Salvatore were side by side watching as Nicolette landed on solid ground. The widow clapped excitedly. "Bravo, Nicolette! My goodness, you have nerve." Nicolette glanced at Salvatore, who quickly hid his concern with a grin and a wink.

"You doubted I could make it?"

"I would never doubt you," he said matter-of-factly, the wind whipping his long, dark hair. "You are an excellent horsewoman and well you know it."

He brought his mount up alongside her mare. He leaned forward and kissed her on the cheek. The sound of approaching horses signaled Darian and Elizabeth had caught up. Darian glanced at Nicolette, his expression indecipherable. He had seemed on edge all morning, and she wondered if it had anything to do with Charlotte's presence. No doubt it put him in an awkward position to be spending one's afternoon with both fiancé and the woman he'd made love to the night before.

For the next few hours the group rode at a slower pace, and listened to Elizabeth's nonstop whining. The woman hated riding and she complained incessantly of her sore back, neck and shoulders.

Darian remained somber, obviously preferring to watch and listen rather than take part in the conversation. However Charlotte proved to be a wonderful companion, telling stories of *the ton* that would make most women blush. It was then Nicolette realized how innocent the duke's daughter was. She did not understand any of the double entendres Charlotte dropped in nearly every sentence.

When finally they stopped to let the horses rest and to feast on wine, cheese and fruit, Nicolette sat opposite Darian and Elizabeth, next to Salvatore and Charlotte. The widow had already divested herself of her boots and now made quick work of her stockings. Darian's eyes flickered over her calves before he looked away.

Elizabeth's cheeks burned crimson. "Lady Mariweather, I find your behavior positively scandalous!"

Charlotte lifted a brow at the young woman. She lifted her full glass of wine. "Here's to you, Lady Elizabeth. A woman of virtue and upstanding morals." She let her gaze fall on Darian for a moment. "Who is the envy of every woman in England."

A nerve flickered in Darian's jaw.

Elizabeth frowned, as though she struggled to understand the toast. Comprehension came slowly and with it another blush. The poor girl would faint if she did not watch it.

Nicolette picked a grape from the cluster and popped it in her mouth. Salvatore sat back on his elbows, looking off to the distance. The sun cast a reddish glow on his dark hair. She released a little sigh. The man truly was perfection. As though sensing her perusal, he glanced at her.

Her eyes searched his face, and for an instant she saw surprise there. Was her desire so obvious then? She smiled softly and he slowly looked away.

Suddenly too hot herself, Nicolette unlaced her boots, rolled down her stockings and went to dip her toes in the small pond.

She heard Elizabeth's gasp and smiled. Nicolette had always loved going against what was considered proper behavior. She almost felt sorry for Elizabeth. For the rules she must adhere to. To her father's strict moral code. He would never let her realize how wonderful making love could be. Though Nicolette was still a virgin, she had been brought up in a whorehouse, and had known that all the sighs and moans had not been acting. Making love could be pleasurable, and she had experienced just the beginning of how wonderful it would be with Salvatore.

"I daresay that the countess would have a fit of the vapors if she were to see you now," Elizabeth said, her face pinched in an unflattering way.

Nicolette glanced over her shoulder and smiled at Elizabeth. "I will try to avoid her at all costs then."

"You forget she pays for your services." The iciness in Elizabeth's tone was unmistakable.

Nicolette was not about to contradict her by telling her they were not being paid. She did not wish to cause suspicion.

Elizabeth sniffed. "I wonder how it is for the two of you, always traveling, always playing for members of the aristocracy."

Salvatore, who had been watching Nicolette, turned to Elizabeth with a frown.

"We have no complaints," Nicolette said, before Salvatore could intervene. She wanted to handle matters herself for once, instead of always having Salvatore come to her rescue.

Nicolette hiked her skirts up higher and stepped in to knee-level. Darian looked his fill and well Elizabeth knew it. The other woman lifted her chin. "How uncertain your future must be. It is well-known that musicians who were popular one Season, are forgotten by the following Season."

Nicolette was grateful for the cool water that lapped at her ankles, and the mud that sucked at her toes hampered her from rushing over and slapping Elizabeth.

"We are fortunate in that we have a following of loyal supporters."

Elizabeth laughed without mirth. "You sound as though you are royalty."

Nicolette thought the duke's daughter most unattractive when she sneered like that. "No, we are not royalty, but I do have the luxury of living like a royal. I go where I want, when I want, and with whom I want. I answer to no one. Not a father, not a mother, not a chaperone…not a husband," her gaze shifted briefly to Darian, "or a lover."

The last was brazen of her, Nicolette knew that, especially when she saw Charlotte's encouraging smile. Salvatore had gone completely still, and Darian looked oddly…pleased. Dear God, she had not meant to entice him, but the little snit had made it too easy for her.

Elizabeth's gaze narrowed as she stole a glance at Darian, who looked at his fiancée with feigned innocence. "Yet for all the success you have achieved, it must be frightening to know that success is but fleeting. Certainly you fear for the future, for tomorrow it could all be over."

Salvatore choked on his wine as he stared at the once-docile creature beside him. No doubt he wondered like Nicolette, how the prim and proper duke's daughter had come by such a devious streak?

Carefully, he set his glass down and met Elizabeth's mocking grin with one of his own. "All things in life are fleeting. You could have all the money in the world, not to mention titles, even beauty, but what does that buy you other than notoriety, things and attention…all of which have nothing to do with you, the person inside."

He lifted a brow. "You have to strip those things away layer by layer, and then and only then will you find the person beneath." A smiled teased Salvatore's lips. "I wonder what kind of person you are beneath that silk gown and those expensive jewels? Would you have the will and determination to make it in such a world, not to mention the talent?"

The hurt in Elizabeth's eyes was obvious. The air was thick with tension, one could easily cut it with a knife. Nicolette glanced at Darian, as though she expected him to champion her. Darian remained silent, his brows furrowed in a frown, his disappointment in Elizabeth obvious.

Elizabeth scrambled to her feet. "Well, I am quite ready to return to the manor. I am in desperate need of a nap before tonight's activities," Elizabeth said, her voice clipped and curt, her brow lifted high as she expected Darian to jump at her command. "Darian, we must go." Elizabeth tried without success to mount the mare on her own. Finally she turned to him, her agitation obvious by her heightened color.

The picnic officially over, Nicolette put her stockings in her pockets, tied the laces of her boots together and mounted with no assistance.

Once they were all in their saddles again, silence ensued, giving Nicolette time to think over Elizabeth's venomous words. She was jealous, that was all. To the duke's daughter, Charlotte's and her behavior must have been a shock. Nicolette had honestly enjoyed Charlotte's brazen behavior, even reveled in it. The woman had already proven to be a wonderful friend, a person she could confide in, a woman who would not judge her.

Like Nicolette, Charlotte rode barefoot. She watched the widow, noticed how she sat with back straight, her chest out. Nicolette mirrored Charlotte's posture. From the corner of her eye she could feel Salvatore watching her. She felt the warm air on her toes, her ankles.

"My lord! My lord!" The cry rang out over the fields.

A child ran toward them, arms waving wildly. His ratty clothes told her he was a servant or a beggar.

Salvatore dismounted and raced toward the boy. Nicolette was fast on his heels. "What is it?"

"Me father's been hurt."

"Where is he?"

"Over there, in the field. One minute he's talkin' away, and the next, he fell to 'is knees. He'd been saying he did'na feel well, but he insisted on goin' anyways."

They followed the boy to where his father did indeed lay flat on his back. At first she thought the man was dead, for he stared straight up at the heavens.

Nicolette moved to the man's opposite side and put her fingers to his neck. Feeling a steady pulse, she leaned down and felt his hot breath against her cheek. The man reeked of liquor.

"Drunk," Nicolette mouthed to Salvatore who nodded. Salvatore put a hand on the boy's shoulder. "You are very brave for seeking help for your father. We will get him home and see that he gets the care he needs. Where do you live?"

"E's okay?" the boy asked, his brown eyes full of tears.

Salvatore smiled. "Yes, he's okay."

Relieved, the boy hugged Salvatore.

Salvatore hugged the boy tight to him. "Now if you would help us by getting your mother."

"I can do that. We live just beyond the hill there."

Nicolette watched with a lump in her throat as the boy grinned and raced for his house. What was it about Salvatore that he could reassure anyone? "You have a gift with children,

Salvatore," Charlotte said, surprising Nicolette. The widow watched Salvatore with a soft smile on her face.

"Salvatore and I can lift him," Darian said, coming up behind them, rolling up his sleeves.

"He is merely drunk," Nicolette said, as Darian went down on his haunches beside her, so close his leg brushed against her skirt.

"What the—" The drunken man stammered, blinking repeatedly. Recognition dawned, his mouth dropped open, and he scrambled clumsily to his feet. "My lord, I didn't know you…that you—"

"Do you make it a practice to work while you are drunk?" Darian asked, his face stern, his voice uncaring.

"I coulda walked," the man said, stumbling back a few feet. "I didna need no help."

Hearing the wagon behind her, Nicolette turned just as the boy jumped from the wagon.

"Papa, you're all right," he said, his face splitting into a relieved smile.

The father said nothing. He just stared past the boy, to the woman who sat silently in the wagon, watching him with disapproval.

The boy was all but forgotten as the man passed by him and climbed into the wagon.

The boy looked so crestfallen, it broke Nicolette's heart. "Thank you," the man's wife said, and without another word, turned the wagon about.

"Come on, boy," the man roared, and Nicolette watched with a heavy heart as the boy ran for the wagon, but stopped short. He backtracked and hugged Salvatore.

Salvatore pressed something into the boy's hand.

He opened his hand, palm up, displaying a shiny coin. "Thank you, sir!"

Salvatore ruffled the boy's hair. "Now go, help your mother get your father into the house."

"E'll be okay?" Worry laced the boy's words.

Salvatore smiled reassuringly. "Yes, he'll be just fine."

"I'd better go before they get angry," the boy said, running after the wagon.

"Well that was disappointing," Darian said, frowning at the wagon's slow progress.

"More than likely it was a one-time occurrence," Salvatore said, walking back to his horse.

"I doubt that," Darian said, with a heavy sigh. "By the state of their clothing, it is obvious he spends his money on drink."

"Perhaps that is why he drinks, because he can scarcely afford food and clothing for his family." Salvatore's voice was stern.

Darian turned, his brow lifted. "Salvatore, you sound so impassioned. Tell me, how do you know so much about a family you have only just met."

Salvatore, already astride the horse with reins in hand, rested his forearms on his thighs. "The boy was truly concerned about his father. If his father was known to drink, the boy would be accustomed to the effects of alcohol, and he would not have been frantically yelling for help."

"But the boy is a child."

"It is amazing how fast one grows up when you are raised with so little."

Darian's lips quirked.

"I can still smell the filth." Elizabeth went so far as to flinch. "How could you touch that boy's hair, Salvatore? Who knows what type of vermin—"

"They are doing the best they know how," Nicolette remarked, irritation lacing her words. "Surely you can't begrudge them that."

"Indeed, you cannot," Charlotte added.

Elizabeth lifted her chin. "I meant no disrespect to you or Salvatore. I realize you came from…similar conditions."

In a flash, Salvatore grabbed the reins from Elizabeth's hands and pulled the horse closer. "You have no idea what it is to live in a place that is cold and damp, to where no matter what you do, you can not get warm. If you had one ounce of compassion, you would realize what it is to live in poverty. As you have referred to many times this day, Nicolette and I have experienced such a life. We know firsthand what it is to go to bed on a filthy cot, your stomach cramping for lack of food. I remember many a day when we went through the garbage of *fine* people like you, looking for scraps to eat, just so we could live to face another endless day."

Elizabeth blinked rapidly as though he'd slapped her.

"You would not survive an hour in such conditions," Salvatore continued, a sardonic smile on his face. "So don't you dare demean anyone who does not have the luxuries you take for granted." He shook his head, opened his mouth to continue his tirade, but instead clamped his jaw shut. Without another word, he tossed the reins to her horse back at her and took off like a shot.

Chapter Seven

ဢ

It took all of Nicolette's willpower to not follow Salvatore. Charlotte had brought her horse alongside hers and leaned forward. "Leave him to his thoughts. Let us enjoy the ride home."

Despite her best efforts not to think about it, the scene between Salvatore and Elizabeth replayed in Nicolette's head over and over again. Elizabeth, at Darian's side, kept her chin lifted high, her fury evident by her rigid stance. Nicolette thought she might ready her things when they returned to the manor…just in case they were asked to leave.

When they had fallen a ways back from Darian and Elizabeth, Charlotte asked, "Have you made love to him yet?"

"I beg your pardon?" Nicolette replied, looking ahead to make sure Darian had not heard.

The sides of Charlotte's mouth curved into an amused smile. "Salvatore. I saw the way you watched him today. The way he watches you. You desire him, do you not?"

It was on the tip of her tongue to deny it, yet Charlotte could read her too well to know she'd lied, and she felt comfortable with the widow. "I do."

She beamed. "I knew it!"

"Yet he does not feel the same."

Charlotte snickered. "My dear girl, you have so much to learn about men."

"What do you mean?"

"I know men. I can read the look in their eyes, can tell by a glance if they want me or not. Just as I saw the way Salvatore looked at you…and he wants you."

The words excited Nicolette, giving her hope. "Yet he treats me like a child."

"He treats you like the child you were, not the woman that you've become. It is time you take matters into your own hands. Show your independence, prove to him that you don't need him—"

"But—"

Charlotte put up a gloved hand. "Let him see that you can thrive without him, and let him chase you."

"He would never—"

"How do you know?"

Nicolette opened her mouth, then snapped it shut.

"The past few nights, as Salvatore's dinner companion, I have learned that the two of you have been inseparable for over a decade. True, you have spent time apart, but never a single night. You have traveled as musicians for five years, and he books you, manages your career, while all you have to do is practice. He is so attuned to taking care of you, he has come to look at you more as a sister, I suppose, than a love interest."

How she wanted to tell Charlotte of the plan to ruin Darian's marriage. Yet she would never betray Salvatore.

"The only thing I do not understand is why you are flirting so outrageously with Darian…and Salvatore seems to condone it. It makes no sense to me."

Nicolette could feel the blush race to her cheeks.

Charlotte laughed. "So I ask you, why do you flirt with Darian when it is clear you prefer Salvatore?"

Did she dare tell her friend the truth?

"I want to make him jealous," she blurted, and Charlotte smiled.

"It is as I thought. You are using one to get to the other. See, you are clever. Let me ask you this. Have you ever been with a man?"

Nicolette shook her head. "No, not like that."

"How far then?"

Nicolette winced. "I have kissed."

"Salvatore?"

"Yes."

Charlotte rolled her eyes. "Let me guess, it was a chaste, on the cheek kiss."

"I asked him to kiss me the other night in the garden."

The widow's eyes lit up. "And did he?"

"Yes."

Charlotte lifted a brow. "Well, tell me everything."

"The other morning I went for a ride and Salvatore came after me. The storm came, both our clothes were wet, so he stood with his shirt off, staring into the flames." Nicolette met Charlotte's smile. "He has a beautiful physique."

"And…" Charlotte prodded.

"I kissed him, and he kissed me back. My hands wove through his hair and suddenly his lips had left mine, to travel down my neck to my breasts."

The side of Charlotte's mouth curved. "And?"

"It felt wonderfully wicked."

"That's my girl," Charlotte said, adding a wink for good measure. "And what else?"

"I could feel—his manhood against me, brushing against my stomach."

"Did you touch him there?"

"No."

"You must. That is the problem with women today. They say nothing of what they want. It is a man's world, Nicolette, but we can take pleasure just as they do. We can tell them what we want and how we want it."

Nicolette shifted in the saddle, horrified yet excited that they were having the conversation. "What if he does not feel as I do?"

"Men want a woman who loves sex. As my mother always told me, be a lady in the eye of the public, but be a whore in the bedroom and always your man will be content. True, some men are intimidated by a strong woman who enjoys sex as much as he does. But I tell you this—a man would prefer a woman of passion much more than one who looks at sex as a duty. Embrace the act of making love. Enjoy the feel of a man's hands on your body, the feel of his cock inside you, hard, pulsing, taking you to a place you never knew existed—to where you can touch the stars."

Blushing at the bold words, Nicolette knew what Charlotte said rang true, for she had felt the ripples of passion as Salvatore had teased her nipples with his tongue.

"If you want Salvatore, you must be the aggressor. He has taken care of you for so long, he has not realized the woman you are. A gorgeous, desirable woman...that other men want to sample. Let him know you desire him."

"What if he rejects me?"

Charlotte laughed. "My dear girl, there isn't a man in all of England who would reject you."

* * * * *

Nicolette found Salvatore in his room, sound asleep, lying on his bed, still dressed in his riding attire, including his boots. She smiled softly hearing his even breaths and seeing the steady rise and fall of his chest.

He had been so furious with Elizabeth this afternoon, and it had shocked her that he'd been so quick to jump to her defense. Always, and especially when dealing with aristocracy, Salvatore kept a cool head. He had learned from a tender age that it was best to stay neutral at all costs, but Elizabeth's words had sent him on a tirade, and he had squarely put Elizabeth in her place.

She had so badly wanted to go after Salvatore, but she was now glad she'd stayed and talked with Charlotte. The woman's candidness was a welcome and surprising change from members of *the ton*. So unlike Elizabeth or the countess who had been waiting for the group, since she appeared on the manor's steps, hands folded before her, watching the four of them dismount. Her brows had lifted to her hairline seeing Nicolette and Charlotte talking like old friends.

Nicolette watched the steady rise and fall of Salvatore's chest. She smiled remembering the feel of his naked chest against her own. Her gaze shifted lower, over his stomach, where one of his long-fingered hands rested in the band of his breeches, to the material that cupped his manhood. Her stomach tightened. Salvatore made a noise and she glanced up, half expecting him to catch her looking at his erection.

Her fingers itched to touch him there, to see, feel, taste him. No doubt he would be shocked to know her secret desires. Suddenly his eyes opened and Nicolette jumped like she'd been shot. "Nic, what's wrong?" He sat up abruptly, looking about the room. "Are you all right?"

She nodded, her cheeks heating. Always he worried about her. When would he come to the realization that she did not need him to father her any longer? "All is well. I thought I would check on you after your heartfelt speech."

The sides of his mouth curved and he lay back down, patting the place beside him.

Needing no more encouragement, Nicolette kicked off her boots and lay down, resting her head against his shoulder.

His fingers stroked her arm, making the hair there stand on end. She breathed in deeply, taking in his spicy, masculine scent. "I could not stay another moment in her company for fear I would do something I would come to regret."

"And here you had thought to charm her."

"I think it is safe to say the charm has worn off. In fact, I've been expecting the countess herself to come escort us off the grounds."

Nicolette put her hand on his chest, feeling the steady beat of his heart beneath her hand. Feeling bold, her hand wandered lower, near the band of his breeches, then up again. She felt his heart jolt and she smiled to herself.

"What happened last night after dinner?" he asked, winding a strand of her hair around his finger.

"Darian drew me into the labyrinth. He wanted me right then and there. Thank goodness Charlotte came along when she did. I passed by her in my rush to return to my room, and found the woman weaving, so drunk was she. I told her that Darian was in the middle of the maze and that he was looking for her. I watched only long enough to know Darian broke his agreement with the duke."

"He had her right there?" Salvatore asked, sounding not at all shocked. "And you watched?"

"Only for a moment. Did you not notice Charlotte's reaction to him this morning? She looked like the cat who ate the canary."

"I wonder where Elizabeth was when that was going on?"

"No doubt snug in her bed dreaming of her future husband."

Salvatore snorted. "The poor fool. He will never be faithful."

"But what of the marriage contract?"

"Men are clever, particularly when it comes to bedding the women we want."

Nicolette went up on her elbow. "And what type of woman do you want?"

His eyes searched her face, as though gauging if she were serious. Apparently sensing she was earnest, he shrugged. "I love all women, which is not surprising given we grew up in a whorehouse. I often felt like we both had thirty mothers, didn't you?"

He was trying to change the subject, but she wouldn't let him. "But certainly there is a certain type of woman that you're attracted to. What color hair, what color eyes? Do you like them slender with small breasts, or voluptuous with large tits?"

"Nicolette!"

She flashed him an innocent smile. "What? Certainly you have a preference."

"What of you, Miss Nicolette? What type of man are you attracted to?"

"Oh no, you don't."

His brows lifted. "I shall tell you, if you tell me."

"I find I'm attracted to tall men with broad shoulders. I also prefer long hair over short."

"Well, that means you are attracted to fifty percent of the population then."

She watched him, drinking in his rare beauty. The smile on his lips disappeared and his eyes narrowed. "What are you up to, Nic?"

Now was not the time to lose her nerve. She had to be strong, just as Charlotte suggested. If she wanted Salvatore, she must make her move and do it now. She cleared her throat. "I want to see what you look like?" He frowned. "What?"

Her gaze shifted to the bulge in his pants. "Down there."

His mouth dropped open. "Nicolette, I think this is going too far."

She refused to acknowledge his shock and surprise, and instead lifted her chin and prayed for courage. "I think it only fitting that I know what a man looks like, especially given the way the seduction is going. I have little doubt Darian will be showing me his cock...and very soon."

He paled as he watched her. "I think you have spent too much time with Charlotte. Things need not go that far. You know that, right?"

She shrugged. "But how can I stop it once it does? After all, I have to lose my virginity sometime, and if I become his lover, then we will have exactly what we want."

Salvatore cursed under his breath. "You must have misunderstood, Nic. Seduction does not mean you have to sleep with him."

"But how can I stop him once we start? Already he is frustrated with me making excuses. I have to get him alone, in my bedchamber, and I will not have you there to save me."

"I will make sure it does not go to such an extent. Make sure you are never alone with him, like you were in the labyrinth. If you meet, make sure you say it is in your room and not his. I will be in my room and you will tell Darian that you will knock on my door, just to let me know you've made it back safely, and I'll be there."

"He believes we are lovers."

"Tell him that I am with a woman, and that is why you choose not to disturb me. That way when Elizabeth does discover him in your room, the both of us will appear innocent." He ran the backs of his fingers along her jaw. "I have to mend things with Elizabeth, but I will make sure she sees you leaving his room. She will run to her father and the marriage will be called off. I am certain of it."

"But how can I escape his advances, particularly when I'm in his room? Already he believes I am teasing him mercilessly."

Salvatore turned his head and kissed her forehead. "I will not let that happen."

A sound at the door startled them both. Salvatore rolled away from her and then strode toward the door. Nicolette stayed where she was, arms crossed behind her head.

Salvatore opened the door and Nicolette had a clear view of Darian and Elizabeth. Darian's gaze shifted abruptly to Nicolette. His brows furrowed. Elizabeth's cheeks blazed red and she averted her gaze, looking instead at the floor.

"Nicolette, I am glad you are here too. Elizabeth has something she would like to say to you both."

Elizabeth quirked her lips. "I apologize for my behavior earlier. I had no right to say what I did. I do not pretend to know how difficult your lives have been, and I did not mean to belittle you in any way."

The words sounded rehearsed, but at least she'd said them.

"I accept your apology, Elizabeth," Salvatore said, glancing over his shoulder at Nicolette.

Nicolette came to her feet. "I do as well, Elizabeth."

Darian's gaze held her pinned to the spot. His dark eyes narrowed slightly. The jealousy she saw there surprised her and made her uneasy.

He cleared his throat. "Well, we obviously interrupted you."

Salvatore did not rise to the bait and instead nodded. "We shall see you this evening. Kedgwick, Lady Elizabeth." With that he shut the door.

* * * * *

Refreshed from a hot bath and a glass of brandy, Nicolette sat down at the card table, intent on winning a hand, undeterred that she was the only woman present, and that the Duke and Duchess of Durham had arrived and watched their future-son-in-law relentlessly.

The duchess, a very plain-looking woman who rarely smiled, had looked down her nose at Nicolette the moment she'd entered the drawing room on Salvatore's arm. The duke had at least smiled, nodded in greeting, then immediately turned his undivided attention to his wife and daughter.

An hour later Nicolette was losing badly and considered quitting when Darian walked into the room. Rather than join the game, he stood back and simply watched her.

Conscious of his steely gaze on her, she wondered what was going through his mind as he silently brooded.

Darian motioned with a slight tilt of his head toward the courtyard. Her stomach knotted. *Did he mean for her to follow?* she wondered, and when he left out the double doors, she waited a few moments before she put her cards facedown and stood. "Gentlemen, I fear I have lost enough this night. Perhaps I will try again tomorrow evening."

Masculine moans filled the air as she took her leave, and discreetly exited a different door than the one Darian had taken.

What did he want?

He was taking a chance meeting her like this. So why did he want to meet now, especially when his in-laws were underfoot, and his fiancée was watching his every move?

Exiting out the double doors, her breath lodged in her throat as Darian grabbed her from behind and pulled her toward the hedge. "Why did you not come to me last night?"

"You were occupied."

His eyes narrowed. "What do you mean?"

"Darian, I am not a fool. I know what transpired between you and Charlotte."

Even in the dark she could see a blush color his cheeks. "What did she say?"

"Nothing. I had been concerned due to her drunken state, so I followed her, afraid that she might fall. That's when I saw the two of you."

His hands tightened on her arms. "It meant nothing."

"I will be your friend, Darian, but that's all."

"No!" He pulled her close to him, and her heart slammed against her ribs. For the first time she was afraid of his anger. "I want you."

"No, you don't."

"And what of the way you and Salvatore behave? You always are touching each other, always whispering, always together." There was no mistaking the jealousy in his tone. "You should hear what people say about the two of you."

She shrugged. "I don't care what they say."

His dark eyes held her pinned to the spot. "What are you to each other? I want to know."

"We are friends, partners, companions."

"Lovers?"

She lifted a brow. "That is none of your business."

"But I would like to make it my business."

"I do not ask you about your lovers."

He laughed under his breath. "You are a witch, Nicolette. Truly, I have never been so beguiled with a woman in my life. Why did I meet you now when I must marry another?"

"Things happen for a reason."

"Do you honestly believe in fate?"

She nodded "I always have. I know that meeting Salvatore when I was a child was fate. I knew the moment I met him that he would be—"

"Do not speak of him anymore. The very thought of the two of you together sets my teeth on edge."

His arms encircled her waist, and he kissed her, his tongue sweeping past her lips, his teeth grinding into her upper lip.

Dear God, was that blood she tasted? Fed up with his boorish behavior, Nicolette kept her arms braced against his. He took a step and she felt her back up against the cold brick of the manor.

On the verge of a scream, his lips abruptly left hers, making a trail down her neck. "This is wrong, and well I know it…yet I cannot help myself."

Her throat was too tight to speak, and it seemed he would not give her time to respond before he kissed her again. "When you are near, I want to touch you, and to know that I cannot is killing me. It's wrong, I know it—" His hands went to either side of her face. "I see desire in your eyes when you look at me, and I don't know if I'm mistaken. Perhaps I'm seeing only what I want to see."

Her heart was beating so loud it was a roar that filled her ears. Where was Salvatore? This was getting too intense and she wanted nothing more than to be inside the manor, safely amongst the other guests. Seeing he waited for her response, she said, "I desire you, as well you know."

The torture that had been in his eyes moments before was gone, replaced by something that resembled relief.

"How can we be together?" he asked, pulling her farther into the shadows.

"Come to my room tonight," she said, the words slipping out before she could stop them.

"What of Salvatore?"

Still he thought that she and Salvatore were lovers. Now was not the time to tell him differently. "He will not come to my room tonight."

"Darian!"

Nicolette jumped at the sound of Elizabeth's voice coming from nearby. "I shall go around to the front, that way she will not accuse you of any wrongdoing."

Darian held her face between his hands. "No, stay here with me for a little while. I don't care if we are discovered. In fact, I wonder if maybe it wouldn't be for the best if we were caught."

"You don't mean that."

Nicolette heard the sound of swishing skirts and light steps. "Please go, before we're discovered."

"Only after a kiss."

She kissed him quickly. "I must go."

"I will come to you."

"I'll be waiting," she said, and a moment later he was gone.

Chapter Eight

ഔ

Throughout the long night, Nicolette had drifted off to sleep, only to awake with a start. Checking the clock on the nightstand only served to remind her the hour was growing late. She had glanced at the wall, wondering if there was a secret wall somewhere, a panel that hid a dark staircase that led from his room to hers.

It had been two in the morning when Salvatore had checked in on her. He had gone downstairs to find Darian and Elizabeth's father playing a game of chess. It appeared the older man was not about to let his future son-in-law out of his sight anytime soon. She had finally fallen asleep and gotten a few hours of rest.

With the dawning of a new day she had much to think on. Last night she had without question expected Darian to show up in her chamber, and Salvatore had been at the ready, to no avail. Now both of them were tired and grumpy.

But she was bound to get his attention this morning, she thought, smiling at her reflection in the full-length mirror. She was pushing convention by wearing specially tailored men's clothing to a hunt. She had the clothes made a few years ago, finding even riding habits too cumbersome, particularly during a hunt. The pants that had once hung loosely now hugged every curve of her womanly body. The shirt with billowing sleeves was as black as her pants and knee-high boots. She stared at the provocative woman who looked back at her.

Salvatore had not seen her in this getup for a long time. Perhaps he would notice today. No doubt she would cause scandal by being so daring, but she had never been one to worry about what others thought—a quality her mother had passed on to her.

As she made her way down the long staircase, she noticed the raised brows of several ladies who exited the drawing room. There were a few who bid her good morning, wide smiles on their faces, no doubt amazed at her audacity.

Salvatore walked out of the dining room with Charlotte on his arm. The other woman laughed at something she said, but then stopped upon seeing Nicolette. The widow lifted her brows and grinned as though to say, "that- a girl."

Seeing where her attention was directed, Salvatore looked up. His eyes widened, and as she descended the steps she could feel his gaze on her—all of her. At his side, Charlotte winked.

When she reached the bottom step Salvatore took her by the hand. "I am absolutely speechless."

"That would be a first."

"You shall have every man panting after you, my dear," Charlotte said coyly.

"Yes, and every woman scowling," Nicolette added, meeting Charlotte's knowing grin with one of her own.

"They are jealous, my dear, for they know you have what they lack." Charlotte laughed. "Not only do they envy you for your beauty, but even more for your daring."

"I wonder if it is too much given the present company," Salvatore said, bringing her attention back to him.

Charlotte smacked him on the arm. "Come, what is the fun in that. I say let her stir up this bunch of old crones. Give them something to talk about."

"That is what I'm afraid of."

"And since when have you ever cared what any of them thought?"

* * * * *

Salvatore had no immediate response to that question. Nic was right. In fact, hadn't he been the one to tell her to thumb her nose at convention, to ignore what anyone thought?

Yet that was before.

Before what? His conscience asked, trying to forget how good she looked in those tight pants, which hugged her curves and showed off how incredibly long her legs were. And her tailored shirt fit her perfectly, accenting her tiny waist and ample chest. Her hair was worn down, the shiny waves falling past her waist in thick curls. One did not have to imagine anything. Her assets were there on display for all to see, and therein lay the problem. He suddenly did not want anyone else seeing her like this.

"Come, let me walk with the two of you to the stables. I do not want to miss this." He extended his arm, and Nicolette took it.

The reaction to Nicolette's attire was mixed. The men smiled devilishly, while the women seemed highly offended at such brazenness. The closer they came to the stables, the more Salvatore wanted to turn and run…with Nic in tow.

Darian, who had been talking with the duke, turned as they approached. The man's dark eyes raked over Nicolette, hot with wanting. Salvatore bristled, calling himself a thousand kinds of fool for coming up with such a madcap scheme of having Nic seduce such a scoundrel.

The duke, seeing where Darian's attention was directed, glanced their way and his gray brows rose to his hairline.

"This is absolutely priceless," Charlotte said, amusement lacing her words. "The duke's face is so flushed, I fear it might explode. Have you ever seen a man turn so red?"

No, Salvatore had not, and as one by one the men turned to stare, he wished he and Nic were anywhere else. Safely back in London, in their townhouse, sleeping the day away, while playing and entertaining the city's elite.

Even the groom who came toward them with horses in tow, blushed to the roots of his red hair. Nicolette, playing the seductress to the extreme, smiled prettily at the boy who was closer to her age than Salvatore, and accepted his offer of help. Nic mounted, and even went so far as to wink at the boy.

"You have your hands full," Charlotte whispered in his ear. "Every man here wants her, and every man here envys you for what you have with her."

Salvatore studied the widow. "Why would they envy me?"

"Because you already have her love, something they would give anything for, and she adores you. She doesn't hide that fact from anyone. Even now Darian watches you like a hawk, wondering what the two of you are to each other. You know the rumors. I know you do. I ask you this, my friend. Have you ever gone out of your way to deny them?"

"No, I have no reason to. I truly don't care what they think."

She lifted a tawny brow. "Or do you prefer them to think she is taken?"

Any response was cut short, for Darian appeared before them. He nodded at Salvatore, then briefly glanced at Charlotte. He seemed careful not to look at Nicolette. He no doubt could feel the duke's eyes boring holes into him.

"Hello, Kedgwick," Charlotte said, a saucy smile on her lips. Salvatore was beginning to truly enjoy the widow's company.

"Charlotte," Darian said, with a curt nod.

Salvatore mounted and turned to Darian. "Will Elizabeth be joining us?"

The duke's dark expression showed how affronted he was that someone as lowbred as Salvatore would ask about his daughter. "My daughter is abed this morning, sir."

Salvatore could not help the grin that came to his lips. Everything he had ever heard about the duke was obviously true. A snob of the worse sorts, whose every look and statement came off as hypocritical of his upstanding moral lifestyle.

"I hope to see her smiling face upon our return," Salvatore said, then with a smile in Nicolette's direction, they lined up along with the others.

A shot fired and the group was underway.

Salvatore stayed close to Nicolette, relieved that Darian and the duke veered off with another group.

Thankfully there were only three days left to the party. If he could just keep Darian away from Nicolette…

Dear God, what was he thinking? He had planned the seduction months ago. Had manipulated their schedule to be in London during this time.

Nicolette turned to him, her smile wide as she raced ahead of him. What would he do if she fell in love with Darian? She was an impressionable young woman who could easily fall under the spell of a young, wealthy English lord.

I want to see you down there?

The words burned his ears even still. True, he had known that a certain amount of seduction would need to take place between his protégé and his brother, but he had not expected Nicolette to be so willing to surrender her maidenhead.

An image of Nicolette beneath Darian came unheeded and he shook his head, as though he could will it away. Even now as she rode the horse, he could see her riding a lover. Her full breasts bouncing, her long hair falling free, like a veil…

For the love of God, what have I done?

Still he could see her expression, when she had awoken and stared down at his cock, the wanting in her eyes. The excitement that brimmed in those luminous depths had been undeniable.

His cock swelled, remembering the heat in her eyes, the feel of her velvety tongue stroking his, the feel of her diamond-hard nipples against his chest, her honeyed walls clamping around his fingers. The pounding of her heart against his own as she found release.

She pulled up on the reins, and Salvatore stopped alongside her. Glancing past his shoulder, Salvatore went still. He didn't have to ask who waited there in the woods.

Darian.

"I am going to go to him. Do not leave."

Though a denial was on his lips, he merely nodded, and watched with a heavy heart as she disappeared into the trees.

* * * * *

Nicolette's heart pounded in her chest. The further he led her into the brush, the more concerned she became. She knew he could easily take her here…just as he had taken Charlotte in the labyrinth.

She glanced over her shoulder, as though expecting Salvatore to follow, but of course he had not.

She had watched him speaking to Charlotte before the hunt, had wondered what they talked about. She knew Charlotte desired Salvatore. Hell, she groped him beneath the table nearly every night, and though Salvatore acted as though he did not want the women, she had to wonder. Who wouldn't want a lady of class and breeding? A woman who took what she wanted, when she wanted, with no care that others gossiped behind her back?

Yet Charlotte herself had given her pointers on how to seduce Salvatore, and the widow herself clearly lusted after Darian.

Darian stopped and dismounted, then helped her from the horse, his hand staying on her waist. She had no choice but to look up at him. "I'm sorry about last night."

She forced a smile. "I waited for you for hours."

"I couldn't get away. His Grace was not about to give me a moment alone, and I didn't help by drinking far too much."

"I think your mother told him about me."

"My mother knows nothing." He kissed her softly. "You have no idea what you do me". His hands, which had been on her waist, cupped her bottom, pulling her up against his thick erection.

His mouth slashed across hers, his tongue stroking hers, deepening the kiss until she found it hard to breathe.

Bracing her hands against his shoulders, she pushed against him. He looked at her wildly.

"I hear someone," she said, relieved when his hands dropped from her.

He looked past her shoulder. "I see no one." He leaned in for another kiss. "Come to me tonight," he whispered against her lips.

"You come to me," she said, noting the intense need in his eyes.

"I will count the minutes until then."

Taking a step away, she said, "We'd better go before people start wondering."

"How will you keep Salvatore away?"

"Trust me, Salvatore will not be coming to my room this evening. In fact, I'll tell him I'm retiring early due to a headache."

"He won't be suspicious?"

She mounted her horse. "He rarely questions me."

Triumph shone brightly in his dark eyes, and Nicolette understood why when she turned to find Salvatore standing there.

"If I didn't know better, I'd say the two of you are having a liaison," Salvatore said, shocking Nicolette. She hadn't heard him approach, which meant he had seen her kissing Darian, had seen his hands on her buttocks, pulling her against him.

His gold eyes shifted from her to Darian.

"Is the hunt already over?" Darian asked, looking anxious to get back with the others.

"Your future father-in-law is quite relentless. I heard no one stood a chance," Salvatore said, his eyes focusing on Nicolette's swollen lips. "In fact, he returns to the manor as we speak."

He looked so intense, his expression indecipherable. She would have thought him happy, ecstatic even...but he appeared anything but.

Chapter Nine

∽

"What do you think of this one?"

Salvatore set his untouched drink on the nightstand, and watched as Nicolette held a gorgeous cream-colored gown in front of her. "They are all beautiful, Nic. Which one do you want to wear?"

Nicolette's brows furrowed. "You always have an opinion about what I should wear."

He shrugged. "Wear what you want, or should I say…wear what you think Darian would like."

She stared at him for a long moment, and unable to keep eye contact he glanced out the window. Huge gray clouds hung in the air, swirling overhead. The weather seemed to match his mood perfectly.

During the hunt he had waited patiently while Nicolette and Darian had disappeared into the trees. The temptation to follow had been too overwhelming and he had followed, leaving his horse behind.

The sight of Nicolette in Darian's arms had been like receiving a blow to his gut. When his brother had let his hands wander over her buttocks, cupping them, pulling her up against him, it had been all he could do not to scream 'no'. Yet he had stood helplessly watching Darian rub himself against her. Unable to watch further, Salvatore walked back to his horse, a million thoughts running through his head. First and foremost, to get Nicolette as far away from Kedgwick Manor as soon as possible.

Nicolette glanced at Salvatore. "You look pale. What's the matter?"

Suddenly thirsty, Salvatore drained the drink and set the glass on the floor. "I am just so weary of being here. You know I was never one for the country."

"That's not necessarily true. You always loved Count de Vassey's property."

"Yes, but given that this is my father's home, I naturally feel unwelcome and most anxious to leave."

"Do you want to go now?"

Was that hope in her voice – in her eyes? Perhaps he was only seeing what he wanted to see.

Nicolette quickly looked away and tossed the gown on the bed. "Perhaps we should just stay in this evening," she said, falling into a chair and pulling off her boots. "Play a game of chess and drink cheap wine."

"What would Darian think when you did not show up?"

She shrugged. "Make him wonder."

"No, we shall go. As to a gown, wear the cream one. It changes colors with the lighting," he said, coming to his feet, and walking toward the open balcony. "It will go nicely with my navy suit. I think it would be a good idea if we let on that we are very much in love. I noticed the duke's expression earlier today when he saw us with Darian. He did not appear happy — not in the least."

Nicolette followed him to where he stood on the balcony overlooking the gardens. Mrs. Stromme stood on the veranda, puffing on a cigar. Seeing Salvatore, she lifted her hand and smiled widely. He waved back. He adored the American woman for her daring. She reminded him of Nicolette.

Nicolette braced the railing as she leaned over. Instinctively he took a step closer. Her mouth curved in a smile, but she said nothing. Instead, she lifted her chin, closed her eyes, and took a deep breath. He stared, smitten. There was no one in the world more beautiful than this woman. Her astounding beauty paled beside her good heart. His gaze slid down to where the man's shirt opened at the neck, showing the rounded curve of her breast. The cool air had stiffened her nipples, the rose-colored nubs pressing against the thin material. His cock throbbed.

"You are nervous," Salvatore said matter-of-factly.

She released a heavy sigh and looked at him. "I know it's silly to fear doing…that, especially when we've talked of such things before, but it's different now than I thought it would be."

Then don't do it!

She bit her bottom lip. "It's just so different than I thought it would be."

"You desire him?" he blurted before he could stop himself.

Her gaze wavered, falling to his shoulder. "No."

"I think you do," he said, shocked at the accusation in his voice. Surprised at how furious he was at the very thought of his brother winning a woman he did not love, but merely desired. A woman who was to good for him. Salvatore ran his hands through his hair. "You actually feel something for him…the one man I hate more than anyone?"

She lifted her brows, obviously surprised by the tirade. From the corner of his eye he noted that Mr. Stromme had joined his wife on the veranda, and their attention was turned to them. Having no desire to be the evening's gossip, Salvatore stormed back into the room. Nicolette followed him, shutting the balcony door behind him.

* * * * *

Nicolette's heart pounded in her ears. She knew she took a chance by lying to Salvatore, and allowing him to think she might desire Darian had been foolish…but necessary.

His fury spoke volumes. It was all she could do not to smile, but instead she clenched her jaw. "You expect me to feel nothing for him?"

He flinched as though she'd struck him. "I cannot believe my own ears." The pain in his eyes made her wince, and she nearly told him the truth, yet Charlotte's voice sounded in her head — *Force him to make a decision where you are concerned. You will know shortly where his heart lies.'*

"I didn't say I loved him, Salvatore."

"Yet you desire him." He ran a trembling hand through his hair. "What is the difference?" His gold eyes held her pinned to the spot.

He released a breath and walked past her toward the door. She was right behind him, uncertain of what to do or say. Never in all their years together had they argued. Sure, they spatted about small, ridiculous things like her playing the wrong key, or which song to play, but never anything intimate.

He was just turning the doorknob when she reached out and put a hand on his shoulder. The muscles beneath her palm tightened but he didn't turn. "I would never hurt you — not ever," she said. "I do find him handsome, and yes, appealing, but I swear to you that is all. I do this for you, Salvatore, because you asked it of me and don't you forget it."

When he turned, the anger in his eyes was still there, his expression intense as his gaze searched hers. Her heart gave a hard jolt as without warning, his mouth descended on hers, and he kissed her with a desperation that shocked her, his tongue slipping inside her mouth, stroking hers.

His strong arms wrapped about her waist, pulling her close. The blood in Nicolette's veins sang, and a heady need filled her, moving low into her groin.

He growled and lifted her in his arms. She wrapped her legs around his waist, and he walked them to the bed, where he followed her down onto the mattress, not once breaking the kiss.

The hard ridge of his cock pressed hard against her woman's center. His lips left hers, trailing kisses down her neck and the sensitive skin between her breasts. With a trembling hand he lifted her shirt from the band of her breeches, his fingers questing as he palmed a quivering globe. Moments later his lips followed, laving her nipple, using his teeth in a way that had her squirming beneath him.

Watching him suckle her was an incredibly erotic aphrodisiac, making her desire reach an unparalleled high. His long lashes fanned against his jutting cheekbones. He grabbed for one of her hands, and pulled it down between them, to rest on his thick erection.

He looked up at her, his golden eyes dark with passion. "You want to know what a man feels like?"

She nodded.

With one hand he unbuttoned his pants and his cock sprang forth, long and thick.

Nicolette released the breath she'd unconsciously been holding.

"Touch me," he whispered.

Her fingers encircled the marble-hard, yet velvety smooth shaft.

Salvatore closed his eyes and moaned, and if she'd hurt him. He rolled onto his back, and she went up on her side, looking her fill of him, her fingers stroking the length of him.

Gritting his teeth, Salvatore watched Nicolette as she looked at his cock in wonder. Sweet Jesus, did she not know what that look could do to a man, particularly when her unskilled fingers ran up and down his length, then biting into her lower lip, she wrapped her fingers tight about him. Swallowing a moan, his fingers covered hers, guiding her.

Her eyes widened in surprise as he grew even longer, thicker and harder. "Amazing," she said on a whisper. His sac tightened, lifted, and he knew if she continued he would give her more of a lesson than intended.

With a growl he rolled away from her, and came to his feet. With trembling hands he buttoned his pants.

"What did I do wrong?" she asked, and when he turned she was on her knees in the middle of the bed, her expression one of disappointment. "I—"

"You did nothing wrong. I let it go too far."

She scrambled off the bed and was before him in two strides. "No, I want you to teach me. Show me how to make love."

He would not show her how to make love to his brother. Already he knew she'd be a skilled learner—a woman who would bring a man to his knees. Looking at her now, her flushed face, her lips swollen from his kisses, her erect nipples thrusting against the fine material of her shirt. He reached out to her, palming her chin in his hand. "You will know, Nicolette. Let your body guide you."

Her brows furrowed, and he knew she didn't like the answer. She placed her hand over his. "I want you...to show me."

If only...

He forced a smile. "We are already late for dinner. You had best get dressed. I shall return in half an hour to escort you."

She let her hand drop to her side. He leaned in and kissed her, a chaste kiss, unlike the one a moment before.

There were a million things he wanted to say, but he couldn't find the courage. His emotions were in turmoil and he wondered if he even knew what he wanted. Without another word, he left her.

* * * * *

Nicolette approached the piano and sat down on the bench. She ran her fingers over the keys softly.

The Duchess of Durham had requested a song be played in honor of her daughter's engagement to the Earl of Kedgwick. The devil in Nicolette wanted to play a dreary, doom-filled ballad, something that signified her mood as well as the impending marriage of Darian and Elizabeth, who stood hand in hand watching with the others.

Elizabeth's serene smile didn't fool Nicolette for a minute. The woman hated her and wanted her out of their lives as soon as possible, and how could she blame her? Darian on the other hand, watched her intently, no smile, no expression whatsoever. No doubt he had learned to school his features for his mother and in-laws' benefit.

In just a few short hours Darian would come to her room. She had no idea how far things would progress before Elizabeth made her "unexpected" visit. She hoped it was not as far as things had gone with Salvatore today. Her heart still hammered, remembering the feel of his cock in her hand, the hard, velvety texture that even now made her stomach tighten, and caused a deep, throbbing ache in her womanly core.

God, what would happen if Darian wanted her to touch him that way? Did she have the courage? And what would she do if he touched her as Salvatore had? Her nipples, where his mouth had been, were still sensitive against the bodice of her gown. Tonight she had pulled out all the stops, wearing the cream-colored gown with a corset but no petticoats.

If she were smart, she would leave now, while there was still time. She should run and forget the day she had ever planned such a devious scheme.

Salvatore came up behind her and whispered in her ear, "How about something sweet and dynamic. Something that will make the mothers incredibly happy."

She swallowed hard. His hot breath stirring her hair made her yearn for more of what she'd experienced in his arms.

"Like our version of Bach's *Overture to a Marriage*?"

He kissed her on the cheek before taking his place center stage. With his nod she let her fingers drift over the keys. For the next few minutes, she let every bit of aggression she felt out on the ivory and ebony keys, giving the song her all. Though she usually closed her eyes while she played, this time she watched Salvatore, not taking her eyes off him, even for a moment.

In turn, he watched her, his bow stroking the strings, like his fingers had stroked her earlier in her room. His eyes were intense, and she could sense the silent question, *What are you doing?*

The side of her mouth lifted slightly, and she increased the tempo, forcing him to catch up. Sweat beaded her brow, but he did not falter, and instead began the game of slowing things down—only to have her pick them up. He always had to have the control when it came to their music…when it came to their lives.

He had almost lost that control earlier today when she had touched him. She could see the passion in his eyes—the intense need—like he could lose himself in her. Her gaze shifted from his, slowly descending. She could feel him watching her in return.

Her gaze stopped just at the band of his pants, then abruptly swung back to his face.

Was that amusement in his eyes? Suddenly he looked at something beyond her shoulder and his hand stopped in midplay—but only for an instant, missing a note…that no one else noticed, save her.

She did not want to look, too afraid of what she'd find, and waited to do so until the final note. The crowd jumped to their feet and Nicolette stood and took the hand Salvatore offered. He kissed her fingers, then leaned forward. "Your father is here."

He could have said anything else, and she would not have been shocked. But she had never expected to hear those words. Salvatore's eyes locked with hers and he squeezed her hand.

Curtsying to the crowd, she nodded to the duke and duchess, then let her gaze swing to the right. Her pulse skittered alarmingly as she stared into the familiar blue eyes of the man she never thought to see again. The marquess was older now, but he had not changed much aside from being heavier set, and his auburn hair had gone gray.

At his elbow was a woman, no doubt his wife…the woman who had taken him from Nicolette and her mother. The marchioness stared at Nicolette, her brows furrowed into a frown, as though she couldn't quite place her. Well, it would only be a matter of time, because even though she shared her father's coloring, she resembled her mother.

Charlotte stepped forward and embraced Nicolette. "That was wonderful. You are truly gifted, my friend."

Nicolette nodded. "Thank you." She leaned forward and whispered, "I have a need to refresh myself. Would you come with me to the withdrawing room?"

"Of course," Charlotte replied. She kissed Salvatore's cheek. "I'll bring her back posthaste."

He nodded, and Nicolette let her fingers slip from his.

They walked in silence until they were in the withdrawing room, which was thankfully empty, save for two elderly women who talked amongst themselves.

"The two of you melted every heart in that room. Truly, the way you watched each other had everyone wishing they were you," Charlotte whispered. "I am absolutely amazed that you are not lovers yet."

How she wanted to share the events of the afternoon with her friend, yet she couldn't. She did not want to sully what had happened.

"Okay, if you will not tell me, then let me ask you this—who is Lord Wellesley to you?"

Nicolette stopped in midstride.

Beside her, Charlotte watched her intently. "He is your father, isn't he?"

Her throat was so tight she could barely swallow. "Yes."

Charlotte watched her intently, and then put her hand on Nicolette's shoulder. "The marquess is a wonderful man with a good heart."

"He left my mother and me to marry another."

"I have no doubt it hurt him to do so."

The words felt like a slap to the face. How dare her new friend tell her what she should feel, particularly someone who had lived a pampered lifestyle. "You know nothing of what my mother and I went through because of him."

Charlotte must have sensed Nicolette's anger, for she nodded. "Indeed, I spoke carelessly. Simon is an old friend."

Nicolette could not believe the timing. Her thoughts were already in turmoil over her seduction of Darian, and now with her father's arrival, she felt more confused than ever.

Chapter Ten

ဆၥ

Salvatore wondered how he would tolerate another three days in the company of all these people with whom he could barely stand to be in the same room.

The footman handed him a large glass of Madeira, which he nursed while trying not to look at the clock again. Where the devil had Nicolette and Charlotte gone? They'd disappeared nearly quarter of an hour ago.

Perhaps Nic had gone to bed to await Darian? Salvatore scanned the room and found his brother talking to Simon Laurent, who kept glancing his way. Did Nicolette's father remember him? He had been just a boy the last time he had seen the marquess.

Before the thought was finished Darian and Simon were walking toward him.

Salvatore steadied himself and took another drink. Darian smiled and extended his head. "Well done, Salvatore," he said, speaking like they were lifelong friends. How fickle those of *the ton* were.

"Thank you," Salvatore replied, finally glancing at Simon. Nicolette had her father's eyes. "Salvatore, may I present Simon Laurent, Marquess of Wellesley." Simon extended his hand and Salvatore took it.

Salvatore nodded. "A pleasure, my lord."

"You are a talented musician, Salvatore. As is your partner."

"What she would give to hear those words," Salvatore said, releasing the other man's hand, finding it rather unsettling to look into the same eyes as his partner.

"They had been playing throughout Europe these past five years. It is only recently they've found rousing success here in London," Darian added.

"Where are you from originally?" Simon asked, brow furrowed.

Immediately on his guard, Salvatore considered lying, but knew it would only make him look guilty. "Originally from London."

The side of Simon's mouth lifted in a smile. "I have spent my entire life in London. I've always enjoyed the city."

Salvatore took another sip of his drink. "I prefer Paris myself, as does my partner."

At the mention of Nicolette, the marquess straightened. "I would very much like to meet your partner."

Salvatore's heart missed a beat seeing Nicolette. "Well, then you are in luck, for she is coming this way."

The marquess seemed to pale. Salvatore smiled at Nicolette, who kept her gaze level with his. He extended his hand and she took it. She trembled. "You are just in time to meet the new arrival. Nicolette, may I present Simon Laurent, the Marquess of Wellesley."

Nicolette nodded and curtsied. "Lord Wellesley, it is an honor."

Simon searched her face, his lips curving into a smile. "You have the look of your mother."

Salvatore squeezed her hand tight, in quiet reassurance.

"Thank you, my lord," Nicolette replied.

She stiffened when her father kissed her hand softly.

"I have waited a long time to meet you."

Darian suddenly appeared perplexed with the situation. "Tell me, how is your lovely wife?" he asked, breaking into the conversation.

Salvatore smiled inwardly. Obviously Darian had misinterpreted Simon's interest in Nicolette.

Simon released Nicolette's hand and turned to their host. "Henrietta is fine, as always. She wishes to travel to Italy come spring, while I return to London for the Season."

"Excuse me, gentlemen. Nicolette." It was Darian's mother, who exchanged a curt nod with Simon. "Elizabeth is not feeling well. Darian, could you see your fiancée to her room?"

Salvatore glanced over where Elizabeth sat with her parents. She indeed looked rather pale. "Of course. Will you please excuse me?"

"It has been a long day. Salvatore, will you see me to my room?" Nicolette asked, a touch too quickly. "My lord, it was a pleasure to meet you."

Without another word, she all but dragged Salvatore toward the door.

"Tell me what you're feeling?" Salvatore asked, worried at her pallor.

"I want this day to be over. The sooner the better." She stopped outside her door and managed a small smile. "Just make sure you don't leave us alone for too long."

"I promise."

* * * * *

Nicolette sat up in bed, her emotions in turmoil. Her father's presence made everything so complicated. She hated that she was second-guessing herself and her reasons for continuing on with this seduction of Darian Tremayne.

Salvatore had noticed Simon Laurent's arrival as well, having remembered him from the theater at which his mother and Nicolette's mother had performed. Simon had been a regular visitor, and Salvatore had recounted the moments when the marquess would bring him a treat, pat him on the head, then tell him to find something to do, as all the women used to share a small room.

Which meant that Simon Laurent certainly knew who Salvatore was. Though he'd been a boy back then, Salvatore was easily recognizable by his exotic looks, and golden eyes. It wouldn't take long for the marquess to put two and two together. He knew Darian well, that much was obvious, and he knew Darian's father even better. They had run in the same circles, courted women together, and no doubt he would think it strange that Franklin Tremayne's illegitimate son would come calling at Kedgwick Manor.

Nicolette's stomach twisted into a tight knot. They would be discovered. Perhaps right now, at this very moment, her father was telling Darian everything. Salvatore had told her not to worry...yet she couldn't help be concerned.

Perhaps it would be wise to abandon the seduction. She started for the door, intent on talking to Salvatore about it.

A soft knock stopped her dead in her tracks. She glanced at the clock on the mantle. It was still too early for it to be Darian, which meant it was probably Salvatore. Maybe he was here to tell her they needed to leave.

Or, dear God, would it be her father come to talk to her privately?

She grabbed her robe, put it on and walked toward the door, pushing her fear aside with every step. Reaching for the handle, she took a deep breath and opened it.

Her breath left her in a rush.

Darian stood before her, his jacket unbuttoned, and his hair disheveled, as though he'd been running his fingers through the short, raven locks.

Damn! It was far too early! Nicolette glanced at Salvatore's door, hoping against hope it would open and he would step out.

Darian's gaze slid over her. "I know it's before the appointed hour…"

Hearing a door open down the hall, he pushed her inside and shut the door behind him. He reached out and grabbed her, his mouth slanting over hers, his tongue sweeping past her lips.

He pulled away just enough to look into her eyes. "From the first moment I saw you, I hoped to have you. Now, I don't want this night to end."

Red-hot fear raced through her. "You were not to come until midnight."

"I could not wait another minute." His hands were at the fastening of her gown, already unbuttoning it.

She jumped away. "I think later would be better."

Darian frowned. "What game do you play, Nicolette? Are you meeting another man?"

"No!"

"Lord Wellesley perhaps?"

She flinched. If only he knew. "Definitely not." She braced her hands against his arms. "I wanted to prepare myself for you."

"There is no improving on perfection, my sweet."

A moment later she was swept up in his arms, and he was striding toward her bed…just as Salvatore had done earlier that day. The difference was that with Salvatore her body had hummed, her hands seeking his body, wanting to experience everything he had to give her. Now, with Darian she felt dirty, not at all good, and she pushed against him so hard, he dropped her to her feet, and stumbled back.

"What is this about?" he asked, his expression teetering between disbelief and rage.

She swallowed hard, her mind clamoring for any excuse. "I did not…"

The door opened against Darian's back, but he blocked it with his boot.

"Nicolette!" Charlotte's voice called from the other side.

Thank God!

She looked to Darian, who shook his head, imploring her to silence.

"Yes, I am here!" Nicolette called.

Darian closed his eyes.

"Then for heaven's sake, open the door," Charlotte said, as the doorknob turned once more.

Nicolette walked toward the door, Darian's eyes narrowed. "Do *not* open that door," he said under his breath.

"I have to."

"Nicolette…" Charlotte's voice was full of trepidation.

His eyes were imploring.

Nicolette sighed. "Charlotte, I am fine."

"Phooey, open the door. I have something to share with you."

Nicolette reached for the doorknob again, but Darian shook his head. "Do not open it," he whispered.

"Hide," Nicolette said with a forced smile. Darian's eyes searched hers, and realizing she wasn't about to give in, he walked toward the window, where he disappeared behind the velvet drape.

Releasing an unsteady breath, Nicolette opened the door. Charlotte's brows were practically to her hairline. "If I didn't know better, I would say you were having a liaison, my dear."

She looked toward the curtain and Charlotte's eyes lit up, and Nicolette mouthed the word "Darian". Charlotte pursed her lips. "I just passed Salvatore in the hall. He said you weren't feeling well, so I thought I would come and check on you myself." Charlotte stepped past Nicolette and walked toward the balcony, just a few feet from where Darian stood. "What a beautiful night it is."

How she loved this new friend of hers.

"Yes, it is."

"You know, I am growing weary of being in this house with all these old fogies. Give me London any day of the week…."

"It is not so bad."

Charlotte sighed. "Perhaps it is the arrival of the duke and duchess. They look down their noses at everyone. When I just passed them in the hallway, they were asking me if I knew Darian's whereabouts? The duchess would not even look me in the eye. Instead, she glanced at the low décolletage of my gown, then fanned herself as though she would faint."

"She does not approve of me either."

"She seems to forget that she and my mother were good friends, and I know all about the hell she caused in court." Charlotte snickered good-naturedly, while rolling her eyes. "By the way, do you happen to know where Darian is off to? I believe the countess is having the servants scour the house as we speak. I would hate to see him come up missing during this most grand event."

Darian stepped out from behind the curtain and Charlotte feigned surprise. "Why, Darian, what in the world are you doing here?"

Looking irritated, Darian ran a hand through his mussed hair. "Dearest Charlotte, though I have the feeling you knew all along I was here, I will take the higher road and ask for your silence in this matter."

Charlotte's lips quirked. "Darling, this will be our little secret, though you should know better than anyone that servants have a tendency to talk…especially servants who enjoy having their hands greased."

Darian looked affronted. "My staff is loyal."

Charlotte lifted a brow. "Come, Darian, everyone has a price. You know that."

"And you?"

Her gaze shifted from his, moving slowly downward. Nicolette could not believe the brazenness of the woman, but secretly applauded her for such daring.

Darian did not share her good humor. If looks could kill, Charlotte would be dead. "I had better go," Darian said, stepping past them. "Charlotte, would you be so kind as to check the hallway?"

"You want me to be your accomplice?" she asked, managing to sound shocked. The woman could give the most seasoned actress a run for her money.

"I ask you to do what any friend would."

Charlotte shrugged. "Very well, but I am only slipping into the hall for a moment. I suggest you stay out of the way in case someone comes barging in here unannounced."

Charlotte swept into the hallway and Darian took Nicolette by the shoulders. "I do not know if we will ever find the time to be alone, but know this much, Nicolette. We are not finished here. Not by half. I want you in my bed, and in my bed you shall be." It looked like he was about to kiss her—when Charlotte walked back into the room. "The hallway is clear, but the duke is down on the first-floor landing. Perhaps the servants' staircase would be a better route."

"Thank you," he said, slipping out the door, no doubt heading for the servants' staircase.

Nicolette shut the door behind him and breathed a heavy sigh. "Thank God!"

Standing in the middle of the room, Charlotte watched Nicolette intently. "Tell me what's going on, Nicolette. I do not understand why Darian was here, particularly when you told me you were quite interested in your partner."

There was no jealousy in the other woman's voice or expression—just honesty.

Charlotte crossed her arms, pushing her generous cleavage to her throat. "Your lips are swollen from his kisses."

Unable to meet her steady gaze, Nicolette blurted, "He wants me."

"And? Do you want him?"

"This is quite awkward, Charlotte. I know the two of you are lovers."

Rolling her eyes, Charlotte released a heavy sigh. "We are all adults, my dear. Darian and I made love. That does not make us lovers, and believe me when I say it wasn't the first time, and it won't be the last. There are few people in your life that you will be attracted to in such a way that when they enter the room, all you are aware of is that one person. Everything else fades away, until you can think of nothing but being with him, having him, making love to him until your bones feel like hot butter."

"You love him?"

Charlotte nodded, and her rouged lips curved. "We met when we were both children. Our families were good friends, and we learned early that we enjoyed each other's company." She winked. "We are attracted to each other, but we are far too alike to be together, and I knew that loving him would be folly for me. I always knew he would marry someone younger than myself, a virgin from a good family. My father had lost our fortune by the time I had come of age. Thank goodness, Charles did not care about money and asked for my hand because he loved me."

Nicolette sat down, and motioned for her friend to do likewise. "And, did you love him?"

"I cared for Charles, and in time I grew to love him, but in a different way than conventional love. He was more than twice my age, and in truth, he treated me more like a pet than a wife. We rarely made love, and he never guessed that I kept lovers. I would never openly hurt him, and I was always discreet. That is until Darian came along." She ran a finger along the embroidered edge of a pillow. "It was the night of the countess's fiftieth birthday and Darian had returned home from university." Charlotte's smile was melancholy. "When I saw him, I swear to you, Nicolette, that my heart literally slammed to a stop. He caught my gaze from across the room, and I felt that wicked grin all the way to my soul."

Nicolette knew exactly how she felt—for that's how she felt when she saw Salvatore.

"Within an hour we were in the drawing room making love. The intensity of that moment still makes my heart leap."

Nicolette could very well imagine. Just as her heart had leapt this afternoon when Salvatore had touched her....

"It was the first time we had made love, and I knew that once would never be enough. We were so young...and so wild." Charlotte took on a faraway look. "Charles walked in on us, and I shall never forget the expression on his face. He was so hurt, and I could do nothing, laying there, my gown up around my waist, my lover between my thighs."

"What did you do?"

"I could do nothing. As horrible as it sounds, the minute the door closed we continued, making love with an intensity I have since never experienced. In truth, I think it made Darian even more aroused to have Charles catch us." She sighed. "That night I knew that Darian would always have a piece of my heart. No one else can make my blood stir the way that man can."

"What did your husband do?"

"When Darian and I finished, I walked directly to my husband's side, and he behaved like he had not witnessed his adoring wife making love to another man." Charlotte shook her head. "I swear to you, Nicolette, Charles did not treat me any differently. He still treated me with open adoration and

A Dangerous Game

doted on me. Not once, even on his deathbed, did he bring up my infidelity. I love him even more for having done so."

Nicolette thought Charlotte's husband a saint. She did not know of any man of her acquaintance who would be so forgiving, particularly walking in on the act itself. Darian should have been called out in a second.

"Would you marry Darian now if he asked you?"

Charlotte's brows furrowed. "Nic, you are daft. Darian would never marry me."

"Perhaps if it were his choice, he would."

Charlotte laughed, but for all the humor in her eyes, Nicolette also sensed an infinite sadness. Nicolette herself knew what it was to love a man who would never truly be hers. Darian desired Charlotte, that much was true, but he would not, for whatever reason, give his heart to Charlotte—much like Salvatore would never give her his heart. He thought love a fickle notion, left for poets and novelists.

Standing, Charlotte shook her head. "What I don't understand is why I am telling you all this, especially about the man who was hiding in your room."

"I don't want him, if that's what you're wondering."

"You want Salvatore, am I right?"

Nicolette nodded. "You know I do."

Charlotte extended her hand to Nicolette. "Then you shall have him. I shall help you into bed, and then I will get Salvatore to come check on you in a little while. Tell him you do not feel well and that you would like him to lay down beside you and keep watch over you."

"He will know that you lie."

Chuckling under her breath, Charlotte smiled wickedly. "You forget, my friend, that I know men well. We women are devious creatures when we want to be. A man needs to know that a woman depends on him for his strength and security."

"He does?"

She nodded. "Salvatore knows that you need him—that goes without saying. He watches you constantly, making sure that you are all right. I swear during dinner, he paid more attention to your conversation than his own."

"He does it out of habit. I've depended on him my entire life. When my mother died, I had no family. The madam wanted to send me to a nunnery, but Salvatore and his mother refused."

"Was his mother kind?"

Nicolette smiled, remembering the gypsy woman with olive skin and gorgeous silky hair—much the same color as Salvatore's. "She was kind, but rarely there when we needed her. Salvatore and I had our own room, up in an old attic space that had one time been used as a closet. We were glad to have it, and each other."

Charlotte began unbuttoning Nicolette's gown. "No wonder you love him like you do."

Nicolette smiled, and allowed the older woman to undress her until she stood in nothing save her chemise.

Charlotte motioned toward the vanity. "Sit and let me brush out your glorious hair."

Nicolette felt a bit odd having her new friend fawn over her. She had never had a relationship with a woman, even her mother had been distant. In truth, she had starved for such affection, but instead had received pats on the head by the whores of the boarding house, where she had been looked upon as more of a hindrance than anything.

When finished, Charlotte set the brush down and pinched Nicolette's cheeks.

"That hurt," Nicolette said, frowning at her friend in the mirror.

Charlotte rolled her eyes. "Beauty takes work, my dear. Men think it comes naturally. If only they knew how we toiled before the mirror. Look at you, Nicolette. There is not a man in all of England who would not want you." She dabbed rose oil behind her ears.

Nicolette looked at herself in the mirror and saw a stranger. Her hair, which she usually plaited before sleep, shone silky and bright, and her eyes looked enormous in her face. Her cheeks were pink, her lips as well. Charlotte leaned forward and yanked on the chemise, bringing the neckline down and exposing the tops of the firm globes of her breasts. Her nipples nearly rose above the lace collar.

"Now lay down. I shall go inform Salvatore that you are not well, and that I had been sitting with you but must be off to bed myself."

"But what if Darian comes back?"

Charlotte lifted a brow. "I will make sure he is kept busy." She smiled. "Now remember, you are the temptress. Let him believe you need him, and then weave your spell over him. I guarantee it works every time."

The door closed behind Charlotte, and Nicolette immediately blew out the candle.

The door across the hall had no more closed when suddenly there was a tap at the door, and it opened.

With heart pumping loudly, Nicolette feigned sleep.

The mattress dipped beneath his weight, and suddenly she felt a hand on her forehead. She slowly opened her eyes. "Salvatore, what are you doing here?"

"Shh," he said, his brows furrowed in concern. Through the window, the light from the moon shone upon his features, and her heart gave a jolt. His cheekbones jutted out as he pursed his lips, a habit when he concentrated. Still dressed as he was earlier, save for his jacket, she realized he had been on the alert, waiting for midnight.

"Charlotte said you were not well? I wondered at the duck that had been served. It did not taste right. Perhaps that is what makes you ill?"

"I don't know."

"Your cheeks look flushed, though it is hard to tell with no light."

"Lay beside me."

He nodded. "Of course."

Thankfully, he did not ask about Darian, and instead kicked off his boots and lay down beside her. He lay flat on his back, and she inched closer to him, nuzzling against him, laying her head on his shoulder, and a hand on his chest. She could feel the unsteady beating of his heart against her palm, and wondered if she was the cause of it.

He ran his hand through her hair, and her eyes closed. "Tell me if you feel like you will be sick." He sat up a little. "Perhaps I should get a basin—"

"No, do not leave me."

He lay back down and she closed her eyes, relaxing.

For long minutes she lay still, not daring to move, taking in the feel and scent of him. How comforting it was to have him near. How many times had they lain like this? Hundreds, yet now it seemed so different. *He* seemed so different.

It wasn't until she heard his even breathing did she dare open her eyes. Expecting him to be asleep, she instead found him watching her.

"I didn't mean to wake you," he said, his eyes searching hers.

"You didn't."

"Do you need the basin?"

She shook her head. "No."

He nodded. "Close your eyes. Sleep."

She could not sleep if she wanted to. Not with him near. If she could have her way, she would stay like this for eternity. She reached up and ran her finger along his jaw. The muscles in his shoulder contracted beneath her cheek. "Thank you for taking care of me."

The sides of his lips curved in a soft smile. "You do not need to thank me."

"I know I don't need to, but I want to."

His throat convulsed as he swallowed hard, his gold eyes unwavering.

Nicolette turned her face and kissed his neck. He tasted salty, yet sweet, and she kissed at the pulse that beat wildly in his throat, then further up by his ear.

"Nicolette?" The word was questioning, yet warning her at the same time.

"Shh," she said, kissing his clenched jaw and high cheekbone. Her hand wandered from his chest, to his stomach, splaying there against the hard planes of muscle. His stomach tightened beneath her fingertips and his breath left him in a rush.

"Nicolette—"

She kissed him, her lips opening, her tongue seeking entrance. He did not disappoint, and with a moan, pulled her on top of him, his hands moving down over her back, her buttocks, a hand weaving through her hair, anchoring her there.

Her heart soared to the heavens, feeling the hard evidence of his desire against her stomach. He pulled the chemise up, his fingers stroking a path up her bare hip. With a growl he sat up, bringing her with him. He wrenched the chemise up and over her head, and tossed it aside. She sat astride him, naked as the day she'd been born, and his hot gaze swept over her possessively.

He opened his mouth as though to say something, but she shook her head, and instead ripped the shirt from his pants and brought it up and over his head, to join her chemise on the floor. With a deep-throated moan, he reached up and pulled her face down to his.

The feel of his chest against her breasts was nothing short of heaven, and as he kissed her hard, she shifted her hips. She wanted him inside her.

He immediately stilled her hips with his hands. "Not yet."

Not yet? He would not deny her this time.

She nodded in agreement and with a wicked smile he rolled over, until he had her pinned beneath him. His long hair felt like silk on her breasts and shoulders, his lips tasting sweeter than any candy. The feel of his hard shaft pulsing against her heated center felt almost too good to be true.

Salvatore ignored the warning bells going off in his head. He knew he should not be here, doing this, with her. Yet he could not force himself to walk away again. Earlier today he had almost taken her, and she would have let him. Tonight she had planned to make love to his brother, but fate had intervened. When Charlotte had knocked on his door, his heart had dropped to his toes thinking that it might be Nicolette, and that he had been too late. Instead, the widow had told him Nicolette had fallen ill and aside from the sudden flash of concern, he felt vast relief.

With his knees, he nudged Nicolette's thighs apart. His cock pressed against her woman's center, the only thing between them the fabric of his pants.

She lifted her hips, seeking, needing. Her hands stroked his back, up and down, over his shoulders, her fingers splaying, holding onto him like she was drowning, only to move down over his back to his waist, and then to his buttocks.

Sweat beaded his brow as she spread her thighs wider, cradling him, seeking his hard length.

"Make love to me," she whispered against his lips.

With heart pounding nearly out of his chest, Salvatore rolled off her long enough to divest himself of his pants and drawers. It gave him a few seconds to bring some semblance of calm to the heated frenzy he had started. Nicolette watched him, and as he moved over her again, he could see the relief in her eyes, the heated passion, the desire.

His cock, already thick and long, grew painfully hard. How he wanted to bury himself deep inside her, but he wanted her to remember this. To be ready for him. He kissed her lips, then trailed a path down her jaw, near her ear, down her long, swan-like neck.

The pulse there beat in triple time, her back arching off the mattress, offering her firm breasts to him. He lowered his head and flicked his tongue against one rose-colored nipple. Nicolette inhaled sharply and he hid a smile while his hand splayed upon the other breast. Her fingers wove through his hair, anchoring him there, her silent panting spurring him on, causing his need to reach a fever-pitch.

His hand slid from her breast, over her quivering stomach, down to the patch of downy hair between her thighs. His fingers stroked the dewy folds, teasing the sensitive pearl with his thumb, while inserting a finger into her tight, hot channel.

Her honeyed walls hugged him snugly, and as he moved his finger in and out of her, her hips undulated, questing his touch.

He kissed her hard, his other hand finding hers, bringing it to their sides, splaying her fingers with his own until they entwined. He looked down into her face, into her trusting eyes. "We cannot go back once we do this."

"I want you," she whispered, her eyes searching his face. He nodded, kissed her, then guided his cock into her.

Sweat beaded his brow. Her tight channel squeezing his length, her hips lifting, questing, wanting more of him.

"This will hurt only for a moment."

She nodded, and with a single thrust, he broke her maidenhead and filled her to the womb.

She bit down on his shoulder and he welcomed the pain. He did not dare move. Instead, he savored the feel of her heat surrounding him, adjusting to the intrusion. God she was so tight, hugging him like a hot, clenched fist.

Her hands had clasped his back, and now her fingernails dug into his shoulders. She slightly shifted her hips, and he needed no more encouragement. With slow, steady strokes he began to move, watching her face as he increased the tempo.

Her hands on his shoulders relaxed, her eyes widened and her lips parted.

Kissing her, his tongue mirrored the movement of his body, and he could feel her smile against his lips, could feel her body quickening as her fingernails dug into his shoulders. "Oh," she said, her breath leaving her in a rush, her heels digging into the mattress as she lifted her hips.

Her sheath tightened and throbbed around him, squeezing him until he followed behind, with an orgasm that left him reeling.

Chapter Eleven

ॐ

Nicolette made her way downstairs, only to find the dining room empty, save for the servants clearing away dishes. "Where are the others?" she asked a passing footman.

"The majority of the guests have gone afield. An archery contest of sorts, my lady. If I may be so bold as to say that the majority of the women are taking this quiet time to handle correspondence or catch up on their reading."

Having no desire to do either of those things, Nicolette thanked the man and rushed outdoors. Following the boisterous voices toward the back of the manor, Nicolette's gaze swept the fifty guests, looking for one man in particular.

Her heart gave a wild jolt seeing Salvatore, standing not ten feet from Darian, both men standing with feet askance, bow pulled back, their target in the far distance.

Salvatore loved archery. He came naturally to it, since he excelled at darts, a game he played to while away the long hours in their attic room.

At the signal, both men released, and Nicolette clapped with delight, seeing Salvatore the winner, his arrow directly hitting the giant red center.

He smiled graciously to the crowd, then shook his brother's hand. How similar the two men were. Very strange for having been brought up in such different surroundings.

Nicolette approached the gathering, her breath lodging in her throat when Salvatore looked up and caught her gaze. His golden eyes roved over every inch of her before settling on her face again. He smiled softly.

A delicious warmth began in the pit of her stomach and worked its way downward to her most private place. Already she yearned to slip away to her quarters and experience the magic of last night.

The crowd seemed to part and Darian walked toward her in long strides. "You are just in time, Nicolette. The few women who have managed to pull themselves up from their slumber are about to give it a go. How about it?"

Challenge sparkled in his dark eyes, and she lifted a brow. "I would love to challenge anyone, including you, my lord."

Had that been flirtation she heard in her voice? Good gracious she had come a long way in a week's time.

"I would enjoy that very much," he said, motioning for her to ready herself.

With every step that brought her closer to Salvatore, Nicolette told herself to remain calm and pretend that last night had been nothing but a tutorial for her. Yet as she reached her partner, she wanted nothing more than to throw her arms around him, feel his heart pound against her own, and to feel the sweet taste of his lips once more.

"Good morning," Salvatore said, handing her the bow and arrow.

She took the bow with trembling hand, and fought to keep the arrow in place. "Good morning."

"You are nervous?" Salvatore asked, his scent surrounding her, warming her, lulling her.

"No," she said, too soon and he grinned.

"You can beat every one of these women who scarcely look like they can handle a bow."

His confidence encouraged her, and taking a deep breath, she extended her arm, and released. The arrow hit the rim of the outside ring. She did not glance at Salvatore. She didn't need to.

She notched another arrow and stared at the target, concentrating on nothing else. She extended her arm again, and released. This time, the arrow hit square in the middle and applause exploded all around.

"Bravo, Nic," Salvatore said, handing her yet another arrow. "Show them what you are made of."

She did not disappoint, as arrow after arrow hit its mark. She stepped back and watched while Lady Candore shot erratically, sometimes hitting the furthest ring of the target, other times missing the target altogether. While she watched, Nicolette stood at Salvatore's side, more aware of him than the contest going on. She watched him beneath lowered lashes, taking in his beauty, his self-assuredness amongst all these titled lords. Sadly she realized, he belonged here, for all that he thought he did not. He was their equal in every way, and honestly, a better man than the whole lot combined.

Sensing she was being watched she looked up to find Charlotte standing across from her. The other woman's gaze shifted to Salvatore, then back to Nicolette.

Nicolette smiled and felt the telltale signs of a blush stain her cheeks.

"Lady Mariweather," Darian said, causing all to turn toward him. "Would you like to try your hand at besting our current champion?"

Charlotte's brows lifted and she smiled sweetly. "I fear I would be no match for one so young and fair."

The men around her laughed but Darian approached with bow in hand. "Oh come, I know you to be quite good at archery."

"I have not been in practice."

Darian lifted a dark brow. "You are afraid?"

The words held a challenge, one that Charlotte accepted, for she all but ripped the bow from his hand.

The men all shouted their encouragement as she took her place beside Nicolette. Wearing a flattering gown of blue silk, and a tri-corn hat with a huge white feather, Charlotte looked ready for a ride through Hyde Park rather than a day in the country. Pulling back on the string, she released and the arrow hit dead center.

The men went wild. "You have found your match, Miss Nicolette," Darian said, an amused smile on his face.

Only once did Charlotte miss the target, and that was when Lady Candore went into a coughing fit.

"Now side by side," Darian said, motioning for Nicolette to take her place.

Charlotte grinned. "May the best woman win."

Salvatore leaned forward and whispered in Nicolette's ear, "You can best her, I know you can." His hot breath stirred her hair and she nodded.

"At the ready? Go!"

Nicolette released and held her breath as the arrow hit square in the middle of the target. Charlotte's arrow had veered just the slightest bit, and it hit just shy of center.

"You did it!" Salvatore pulled her into his arms and swung her about. She dropped the bow and wrapped her arms about his neck, sharing his smile and his happiness, aware of his body in a way she had never been before.

"Congratulations, Nicolette." Darian's voice was edged with steel, interrupting the moment.

Salvatore set her on her feet and she turned to their host.

"Thank you, my lord."

"Will you be joining us for a ride?" His brows were lifted in question, his dark eyes intense.

"Of course."

He leaned forward and whispered, "I am glad you are not wearing your breeches, for I would have a hard time concentrating on the ride ahead."

By the wicked expression on his face, she knew what type of riding he had in mind.

"I would not want to be held responsible for injuring you."

"Ah, Nicolette. You can hurt me anyway you'd like."

Her cheeks blazed red. Nicolette glanced at the woman who had graciously let her win, and smiled. Charlotte smiled, but it didn't quite reach her eyes.

No doubt Charlotte thought her daft. One moment she said she wanted Salvatore, the next she flirted with Darian. If only she could tell her the truth.

"Come," Darian said, extending his arm to her. She took the elbow he offered, and walked toward the stables, the others on their heels.

"You surprise me, Nicolette."

"In what way?"

The sides of his mouth curved in a smile. "In many ways. Who would have thought a musician, a woman at that, would be so skilled with a bow? You ride like a man, and do whatever your heart pleases. You do not care about the strictures of society, do you?"

"Should I?"

He shrugged. "I think we all have boundaries—some are just broader than others."

"What if you had not been an earl's son? What would you have done with your life?"

He frowned, contemplating. "I think I would have liked to be a sea captain, or perhaps a soldier."

"Perhaps the Royal Navy?"

"No, my father would never allow it. I was the only heir, and he did not want to risk me being killed. I always admired the Duke of Marlborough. He was not only a brilliant soldier, but a very wise business man."

"Indeed, he was. But you know, his wife was very wise and managed the businesses while he was away fighting."

He laughed, the sound low and pleasing, and she smiled up at him. How he resembled his brother. The way the corners of their mouths curved just so. The shape of their eyes, the long, thick lashes.

The smile left Darian's face. "I will go up in flames if you continue to look at me that way."

She dropped her gaze from his, embarrassed that he had misinterpreted what he saw in her eyes. If only he knew he had a brother. "So, you are an only child? Do you wish you had siblings?"

"Of course. I think all only children do."

"Would you prefer a brother or sister?"

His eyes narrowed as he looked down at her. "Well, I suppose I would enjoy having a sister to dote on, though I fear I would be quite overbearing. A brother would be equally nice, though I must say I would want to be firstborn. I have many a friend who are second, third and even fourth sons, who envy their oldest sibling their birth status. I would hate to have such a rift with a person so dear to me."

Nicolette nodded, and Darian pulled her closer. "And what of you, Nicolette? Do you have siblings?"

"No."

"I imagine Salvatore is like a brother?"

She frowned. "No, not at all."

He pursed his lips. "Ah, so I was right—you are lovers."

When he said the words before, she had taken offense, but now she had no defense. Unashamed of her love for Salvatore, she smiled up at Darian. "Think what you will, my lord."

"You will always keep me guessing, won't you, my dear?"

She was saved from replying as they came upon the stables. Darian released her arm abruptly, and Nicolette immediately knew the reason. Simon Laurent had rounded the corner and came toward them, a pleasant smile on his face.

Somehow in all these years she'd built a wall, believing that he could never touch her. "I had best pick my mount before the others join us," Nicolette said, and without waiting for a response, she turned and with a trembling hand, reached for the door to the stables, opening it with more force than necessary. A groom met her with a surprised smile, and as she passed him by, she knew she had to keep her emotions under control.

She went directly to the horse she'd ridden since her arrival at Kedgwick Hall, smiling as it nuzzled her hand. "How are you today, my beauty?"

The stable door opened and closed.

"Miss Nicolette, is that you?"

The marquess's voice sent a shiver up her spine. This meeting had been inevitable since the moment she saw him at the base of the stage. Swallowing past the lump in her throat, she turned and met her father face-to-face. They were alone, and there was no one else to hide behind.

"Indeed it is, my lord."

He stared at her for a long, uncomfortable moment before saying, "You bear a striking resemblance to a woman I once knew. You have the same bone structure, the same beautiful color of hair."

A door opened, and Simon turned. Nicolette looked past his shoulder to see Henrietta walking toward them, her expression impossible to read. "There you are, my darling," she said, her voice rather high, and a bit forced.

Nicolette watched Henrietta closely, wondering again what the woman possessed that had won over Simon. Certainly it was not her looks, for the woman, though slightly attractive, did not hold a candle to her mother's beauty. It had to be money, or social standing.

"Darling, this is Nicolette. Remember, the pianist who played last night?"

"Ah, yes indeed," the marchioness said with a small nod. "You are incredibly talented."

"Thank you, my lady."

His gaze lingered for a moment longer, before he said, "Well, we have taken up more of your time than intended. We shall see you this evening."

When the door closed behind them, Nicolette sank to the bale of hay. There was no question in her mind that he knew she was his daughter. What would be the best action to take? Perhaps she should try to find Salvatore and tell him what had happened. The door opened and closed again, and Nicolette waited for her father to reappear.

"Who is he to you?"

Darian.

Nicolette swallowed hard and forced a smile. "Who?"

He entered the stable and crossed his arms over his chest. "Simon."

Did he already know the answer and was merely testing her to see if she told him the truth? "No one."

He took a step closer to her, his presence towering. "I will not be cuckolded, Nicolette."

Cuckolded! Oh what a cad! "We only just met. His wife was here too."

Darian quirked his lips. "The first time I met you, I realized that you reminded me of someone, but I could not place who this person was, but it has haunted me for days. I think I know what the marquess is to you."

Nicolette swallowed hard.

"He is your father, isn't he?"

She felt like a butterfly pinned to the wall, the way his dark eyes penetrated her, almost accusing. He took a step closer, pulled her up against him. "Why are you here, Nicolette?"

She licked lips that had suddenly gone dry. "What do you mean?"

"Why are you here at Kedgwick Hall? What are you about? One minute you flutter your eyelashes, devote songs to me, kiss me, tell me that you will be my lover, yet when it comes to the act, you find any excuse to beg off." His fingers tightened around her arms. "So tell me, who are you really, and what do you want with me?"

Straightening her spine, she met his gaze unflinchingly. "I think you are a very handsome man, and as you stated yourself—I go after what I want, with no thought of consequence. I saw you, and from that moment I knew I wanted you."

His dark eyes searched hers, seeking the truth, and she did not dare bat an eyelash. Her gaze slid to his lips and she went up on her toes and kissed him.

The grip on her arms loosened, and then he crushed her to him, his lips hard, demanding, desperate.

Her arms encircled his neck, and she forced herself to relax, to do what she must in order to gain his trust and put from his mind any suspicion.

She pulled away slightly, looking up at his dark, wild eyes. "Tonight. No more excuses. No more waiting."

The triumphant smile disappeared as he claimed her lips once more, his hands pulling her against him. "See what you do to me?" He took one of her hands and guided it to his thick erection.

Her hand trembled, and her stomach curled to her throat. How could she be intimate with this man? How could she touch him like she had Salvatore?

An image of her mother and the women from the brothel came to mind. Those women had no choice. Her mother had had no choice. She had given her body because she had needed to, and Nicolette would do the same. She would simply do the act, go through the motions, and tell herself that it had been duty, that her love for Salvatore had made her do just that.

* * * * *

Salvatore did not like the silence.

Charlotte's hand tightened on his arm. Inside the stable she nodded toward the closed stall. From his height, he could see Darian and Nicolette. The two were kissing, Darian's mouth hard on Nicolette's…and she clung to him, her arms entwined about his brother's neck, her eyes closed, her soft sighs telling him in an instant that either she was a remarkable actress, or she enjoyed what his brother was doing to her.

"Tonight. No more excuses. No more waiting." It was Nicolette's voice. An instant later a growl escaped Darian and the two were kissing once more.

"See what you do to me?"

Salvatore did not have to guess what Darian spoke about. His heart missed a beat, imagining Nicolette touching the other man intimately.

Charlotte frowned at the stall door, then before Salvatore could stop her, she pushed it open, pulling Salvatore along with her. Darian and Nicolette jumped apart.

"Oh, you startled me," Charlotte said, putting hand to heart, and looking back over her shoulder at Salvatore, imploring him to play along. "Salvatore and I were just looking for—"

"A quiet place to talk," Salvatore finished for her, noting the guilty look on Nicolette's face.

"It appears the two of you had the same thing in mind." Charlotte turned her attention back to Darian, brow lifted high.

Nicolette stepped toward Salvatore, and took his hand. "Come, help me mount up."

"You have never needed my assistance before," he replied, surprised to hear the jealousy in his voice.

How lovely she was today, her color high, her cheeks flushed…just as they had been last night when he had made love to her. Still he could taste the sweetness of her lips, hear the sound of her sighs as he thrust within her, the heat of her tight sheath, squeezing him, milking him of every ounce of seed. How foolish they had been, especially not to take precautions, but he had not been able to withdraw. Even now she could be carrying his child.

Their child. For a moment he allowed himself the fantasy. Believing that he could bring a child up in the world — perhaps a girl with red curls and green eyes like her mother. He smiled inwardly at the thought, and when Nicolette glanced up at him, his heart gaze a jolt.

Had last night been about tutoring? Had she wanted to seem accomplished for Darian, or had there been more to it? They both learned from an early age that the act of making love had little to do with the emotion of love. His own mother had spent the last fifteen years of her life on her back, servicing men from all walks of life. Her soft cries had filled his young ears, leaving him with a sense of loathing that had followed him into adulthood.

It had been a young whore at the brothel, a friend of his mother's, who had taken his virginity. He had been only thirteen, young and furious with the hand life had dealt him.

While he played the piano one night the whore had slid on top of the scratched Bechstein, her assets hanging out of her top, her eyes hot with wanting.

He had seen the look on other woman's eyes, but ignored it. His looks had always drawn attention—not the type of attention he cared for.

That night he had become a man, and the whore would go on to teach him every way to make love, how to please a woman, where to touch her, what to say.

However, after a time he grew weary of the whore and he turned his passion to music, yet from time to time he would wander into a woman's room and take her up on her offer, just to sate his urges.

But now he knew that it could be different. Making love did involve the heart, and it when it did, it held limitless possibilities.

This morning he had woke with Nicolette at his side, and a million notes had come in rapid succession. He had not wanted to leave her soft body, but he had the urge to write down the notes, to put his thoughts on paper, so he could share it with the world.

So he could share it with her.

"You've ink on your fingers," she said, as though reading his mind.

He looked at where their fingers were entwined, and he squeezed her hand. "I was inspired this morning."

Her gaze flew to his, and her eyes searched his face. He smiled softly, then motioned to the awaiting horses. "Shall we?"

Chapter Twelve

ဢ

Nicolette wanted to scratch Charlotte's eyes out.

From the moment the other woman had mounted her gray mare, she had been no more than a few feet from Salvatore. And it appeared Salvatore enjoyed the blonde's company for even now his laughter rang out about their small group.

Mr. and Mrs. Stromme brought up the back of their small party, while Viscount Athenry and his cousin rode ahead. Darian stayed close to Nicolette's side, and every time she looked up, it seemed he was watching her.

She yearned to increase the horse's tempo, to catch up to Salvatore and Charlotte, but she did not want to look jealous, and she didn't need Darian questioning her further. He already knew Simon was her father. It would take nothing for Darian to learn the truth about Salvatore, especially since it was common knowledge Darian's father had been close friends with her father.

It was with vast relief that they came upon a small village market, and they could dismount. Darian paid a group of young boys to look after their mounts, and Nicolette breathed deeply of the fragrant breads in a nearby stand.

Charlotte took Salvatore's arm and led him off in the opposite direction. The viscount and his cousin went straight for the pub, and Mr. and Mrs. Stromme seemed intent on the baked goods stand.

Leaving Nicolette alone with Darian once more.

"Stay right there," he said, his eyes warm, his smile genuine. She did as he said, watching the goings-on, trying hard not to notice Salvatore and Charlotte looking at jewelry. Charlotte put a ring on Salvatore's finger and grinned coyly. The woman was breathtaking, and it seemed everyone in the marketplace watched her. Salvatore shook his head, and took the ring off and handed it back to the cheerful widow.

Charlotte picked up a necklace, handed it to Salvatore, then presented her back to him, obviously wanting him to help her with it.

While Nicolette watched Salvatore's graceful fingers manage the necklace, his hands on the woman's neck, his long hair brushing against Charlotte's bare shoulders, she felt a rush of anger.

"For you," Darian said, and she turned to find him holding a rose out to her. "I would fill your bedchamber with them if I could, but I fear that would draw undue attention to us, which we do not need."

Nicolette had no right to be jealous of Charlotte. After all, Charlotte had been nothing but kind to her. She had seen the look of disbelief on the widow's face when she had entered the stall to find Nicolette in Darian's arms. She had been confused before about Nicolette's intentions towards Darian. No doubt she thought the worst of her now.

Taking the rose, she brought it to her nose and deeply inhaled the scent. Roses had been her mother's favorite flower, and she would always associate the scent with her. "Thank you."

"You are most welcome. Come, what do you want to look at?"

"How about jewelry?"

Charlotte smiled as they approached. "Look at what Salvatore has bought for me," she said, smiling prettily as she displayed the necklace. "What did you buy?"

Salvatore, who had been paying the merchant, grinned. "Yes, well there is no denying a woman when she has her mind made up."

Charlotte swatted at his hand. "Come, I offered to buy you a ring."

"He does not like rings," Nicolette blurted before she could stop herself.

"Do you not?" Charlotte asked, wrapping her arm around Salvatore's so tightly, her breast brushed against his arm. Nicolette took a step closer to Darian, and fought the urge to do the same.

The difference was that she was boiling over with jealousy, while Salvatore seemed not at all affected.

She lifted her chin a fraction. If he could remain indifferent, then so could she. "Darian bought me a rose," Nicolette said, holding the flower to her nose.

Salvatore smiled. "How kind of him."

"Buy me a rose?" Charlotte pleaded, looking up at Salvatore with her gorgeous blue eyes, which Nicolette yearned to scratch out.

"Of course, my sweet," Salvatore said, winking good-naturedly, playing along to the extreme, motioning to a young girl with a basketful of colorful wildflowers. He gave the girl a coin, a light pinch on the cheek and took the small bunch from her, handing it to Charlotte, who seemed to melt under Salvatore's generosity. Wildflowers were Nicolette's favorite…and well Salvatore knew it.

The afternoon dragged on endlessly, and not once did Charlotte stray from Salvatore's side for more than a second. They left the market, and followed the river upstream, toward Kedgwick Manor. The day was warm, and seemed to grow hotter by the second.

The small group ahead of them stopped along the river's edge and Nicolette laughed when Mrs. Stromme, with Salvatore's urging, stepped into the chill waters, her skirt up to her chubby knees. Mr. Stromme sat on the grassy bank, shaking his head, but smiling widely, obviously enjoying the sight of his wife in childlike mode.

Salvatore held onto the woman's hand, as they maneuvered the slick stones beneath their toes. If possible, Nicolette loved him even more for his kindness to the older woman who so openly adored him. Mrs. Stromme shrieked as a foot slid, and Salvatore braced her with an arm, pulling her into his embrace.

Mrs. Stromme, once she regained her footing, flashed a devilish smile at her husband. "I told you, Reggie, that one day a young man would knock me off my feet. I daresay, that day has arrived."

"And a man so beautiful, I can scarcely compete," Reginald said, winking at his bride of thirty-four years.

Mr. Stromme was right. Salvatore was beautiful. The shine of his long hair, looking a lighter shade of dark brown in the sunlight. His high cheekbones jutted out as he pursed his lips, concentrating on his footing. Memories of the night they spent together flashed before her, and a warmth spread throughout her body, heating her blood, reminding her of the soreness between her thighs, where he had been last night.

Already she wanted to experience it again...and again. Make her blood sing and her spirit soar.

Darian stood nearby, tossing stones into the river with the viscount and his cousin. The three talked amongst themselves, ignoring the rest of them, though Nicolette could feel Darian's gaze on her from time to time.

Charlotte waded out to Salvatore, and Nicolette sat up straighter. The woman's graceful beauty and fiery spirit was something Nicolette admired, especially when both women and men of *the ton* were so quick to judge.

"Why do you not join them?" Mr. Stromme asked, his voice encouraging.

Nicolette grinned. "I am enjoying watching."

"Fiddle-faddle," the older man said, kicking off his boots. "They can not have all the fun."

Needing no more urging, Nicolette kicked off her shoes and rolled her stockings off. Reginald helped her to her feet, and she allowed the older gentleman to lead her out toward the others who were up past their knees now in the cold water.

Mrs. Stromme shrieked again and Salvatore chuckled. Charlotte turned at Nicolette's approach, her smile warmer than it had been earlier today. Nicolette felt horribly guilty for having been caught in Darian's embrace, especially since she knew how much Charlotte loved the other man. True, Charlotte had told her that they were only lovers, perhaps just friends, but Nicolette saw something else in her eyes—a warmth and desire she went to great lengths to hide.

Charlotte took Reginald's other arm. "We will show your wife that Salvatore is not the only charming one."

Reginald grinned widely, clearing his throat loud enough for his wife to hear over the water.

Mrs. Stromme turned, her brows lifted high. "You've come to help your wife who is in distress, I see. You are just in time, my prince. I daresay I can no longer feel my toes for the cold." She leaned toward Salvatore and kissed him on the cheek. "Thank you for looking after me, dear boy, but I will leave you and these two lovely women to discover the deeps of this damnably cold river alone. I fear my age is beginning to show." Salvatore kissed her hand and released her to her husband.

Nicolette lifted her skirts thigh-high, and ventured out further into the water.

"Nicolette," Salvatore said, his voice tinged with warning.

"What?" she said, throwing him a daring glance.

Charlotte hovered behind them, seeming content to stay in the calf-high water.

Nicolette took another step, her foot hitting a slippery stone this time. The next thing she knew, she saw sky and the tops of the trees, and then was pulled down into the river's cold water.

She heard Salvatore yell, then nothing but the rushing water as she was pushed along the rocks, further downstream. The river got deeper, her skirts heavier, pulling her down beneath the swirling water.

Seconds seemed like minutes as she fought to keep her head above water, and soon she could not. She swore she felt a hand grab her, only to let go. *Salvatore did not jump in after her, had he?* The river was relentless, pulling her further downstream, and further beneath the water.

Her lungs were on fire, and she fought for the surface, but to no avail. Black swirled about her and her head struck something hard...and finally a calm came over her, and she stopped fighting altogether.

* * * * *

Salvatore dove into the water right as Nicolette slipped, and every time he had her within reach, the river would take her ever further.

The current took them downstream so fast, all he could do was pray that Nicolette would grab for a rock, a branch, anything! But her skirts must have grown too heavy, weighing her down, to the point she went beneath the water's surface. Time and again she fought to the surface, only to plunge below.

His heart had ceased to beat when she did not come up and panic ensued. He dove beneath the waters, searching for her, and by a miracle of fate, the river had wedged her against a rock cropping.

She did not move, and as he pulled her from the water to the river's edge, there were no signs of life in her limp body.

Though exhausted himself from fighting the current, he straddled Nicolette, placing his hands over her breastbone, pumping, his mind racing. He recalled reading the story of a soldier who had valiantly tried to save his friend who had very nearly drowned.

Salvatore leaned over her, listening for a heartbeat.

Nothing.

Panic paralyzed him for a moment, and he stared helplessly at his beloved. Her face was stark white, her mouth open, her lips blue.

"Is she alive?" Darian asked, racing down the embankment and falling on his knees beside them. The viscount and his cousin were fast on his heels.

Salvatore pushed down hard on Nicolette's chest once more.

Nothing.

"Breathe, damn it!" he screamed, sending birds overhead flying from their nests.

The others raced toward them, their cries of disbelief confirming his worst fears.

Salvatore took a shaky breath, blocking out everything around him, focusing everything on his efforts to revive her. Her body jerked beneath his ministrations.

"I believe she is dead." Darian's somber voice penetrated Salvatore's brain, and he looked up into his brother's eyes, which mirrored his pain.

Salvatore grabbed Darian by the shirtfront. "No, she is *not*!" He pushed him so hard, Darian fell back, but caught himself.

Charlotte reached out to him. "Salvatore, she is gone."

"No!" He brushed Charlotte's hand away, refocusing his efforts on Nicolette. He took a steadying breath and tried again to revive his friend—the woman he loved and adored—the woman whose innocence he had taken last night, a night that would burn in his memory for all eternity.

Still straddling her, he went up on his knees, using the palms of his hands as he pushed hard on her chest. Time and again he went through the motions, stopping every few seconds to put his cheek to her mouth, with the hopes he would feel her sweet breath against his skin.

Nothing.

Silence filled his ears, and he knew the others watched in horrified stillness. He was a man possessed, but he did not care what they thought. He would not give up as they had. He would not lose his Nicolette. He continued with his efforts, stopping only to put his cheek to her mouth in the hopes to hear any sign of life.

Still nothing. Tears burned his eyes, but he blinked them away.

"Sweet Jesus, I cannot bear it!" Mrs. Stromme cried, before she fainted, her husband catching her before she hit the ground.

Dear God in Heaven, help me! Salvatore silently screamed, breathing into her mouth, hoping to coax her back to life.

Nothing. A fear he had never before known ripped through him.

"Do not take her from me!" he yelled his anguish to the heavens for all to hear, shaking with bone-deep fury. The tears that filled his eyes spilled over, and he stared helplessly at the woman beneath him. "God, don't do this. I cannot live without her."

And God answered.

It came in the way of a sputter. He held his breath, and a moment later Nicolette retched river water, her body so weak she could not turn her head, so he did it for her.

Relief rushed through him at the sweet noise. He rolled her onto her side, holding back her hair as she vomited vast amounts of water, her body convulsing with each spasm.

Charlotte began to sob with joy, the men amongst him shouted with delight, and Salvatore dared to close his eyes for an instant to thank God.

When he opened his eyes, Nicolette stared up at him, her green eyes wide with fear—and a haunted look he would not forget for as long as he lived. She had seen death, he knew it...and he had just been to hell and back. A hell he had not thought possible.

Her hand reached up to touch his face, and he turned his head to kiss her palm, covering her freezing hand with his own. Tears brimmed in her eyes, and fell onto her cheeks. The sides of her mouth lifted the slightest bit, her once blue lips now regaining their rose color.

He pulled her into his embrace, his weak arms finding strength, holding her to him, desperate for her touch. Her breath was warm against his neck, her pulse still slow, but steady as he rocked her.

She would be okay.

Chapter Thirteen

ഓ

Nicolette opened her eyes. The room was filled with bright sunlight, which streamed in through the open window, allowing a warm breeze to flow.

And sitting by the window, gazing out, was Salvatore. He sat in a chair, his elbow on the armrest, a long finger moving over his lips—a nervous habit.

She smiled to herself, taking comfort in the fact he was near. Throughout the long night past she had suffered images of her near-drowning, of Salvatore over her, pushing her chest, mingled with memories of their lovemaking. She remembered giving up hope as the water had surrounded her and pulled her down, her lungs nearly exploding, the sweet calm that enveloped her, drawing her away from Earth and its pleasures.

Her life had flashed before her, like a series of pictures, from her as a little girl, and it seemed each memory included Salvatore. Him as a child, taking her by the hand, sleeping beside her on the old cot in the brothel's attic, looking after her, teaching her his beloved music, explaining to her the changes that had taken place in her body when she had gotten her first menses, teaching her to dance...and teaching her the wonders of making love. Nicolette had awoken from the dream with a start, to find Charlotte beside her, holding her hand, reassuring her it was only a dream and to find sleep once more. But now Charlotte was gone, and it was just the two of them.

"Come here," she said, her voice harsh.

Salvatore started, turning to her, a relieved smile on his face as he stood and came toward her in long strides.

Nicolette's breath caught in her throat. He looked exhausted with dark circles beneath his eyes, making the gold irises more prominent.

She took in everything about him, from the breadth of his shoulders, to the narrowness of his waist, down over his long legs. He had foregone his jacket and wore just a white linen shirt, and his favorite navy breeches tucked into polished Hessians.

The bed dipped beneath his weight, and as he sat down, she opened her arms to him.

His lips curved in a smile, and he embraced her, holding her tight.

"You saved my life."

He didn't say a word, just held her, his gentle hands stroking her hair.

She dare not move — too thankful that God had given her another chance. Putting him at arm's length, she frowned. "You're so quiet. What's the matter?"

"I am just tired, that is all."

"You look like you haven't slept at all."

"I've managed a few hours here and there."

"Liar."

He laughed softly, fleetingly, and she knew there was more to his silence than lack of sleep.

A soft knock sounded at the door, and Salvatore got up and walked across to answer it.

"You are awake!" Charlotte said, a wide smile on her face.

"I will allow you ladies time to catch up," Salvatore said, one hand on the doorknob. "I have some things to attend to."

"You're coming back, aren't you?" Nicolette asked, sitting up against the headboard, wincing with the pain the slight movement caused. It seemed every muscle in her body ached.

"Of course," he said, then with a wink he left, shutting the door behind him.

Charlotte rushed forward, leaning over Nicolette to kiss her on the cheek before pulling a chair up beside the bed. "You look much better today. It does not seem like it has been two days."

"I can not believe it's been two days either."

"You gave us such a scare." Charlotte's voice wavered, and she put her hand to her lips. "I am sorry, my dear. The memory is forever etched in my mind. I can not close my eyes without the horrible image of you laying there, looking like death itself."

"I vaguely remember."

"He brought you back from the dead, Nic. I swear it. You were not breathing, and God forgive me, but I thought you were dead. We all did, but Salvatore would not hear it. He would not stop in his efforts, and I am forever grateful for his perseverance." She pulled a kerchief from her dress sleeve and dabbed at her eyes. "That man loves you, Nicolette, with an intensity I have never seen. I saw raw pain in his eyes, heard the fear in his voice as he asked for God to help him. He roared it to the heavens. I tell you the very hair on my arms stood on end — and still does just thinking of it. When you stirred, I knew that I had witnessed a miracle."

Nicolette smiled softly. "I am well, and it is behind us."

"Forgive me for being so mean to you that day. I confess that I was angry with you for being with Darian. I did not understand, and though I still don't, I had no right to be cruel. I blame myself, because I doubt you would have ventured into the river so far. I can not imagine if you had died, Nicolette. I would live with the guilt for all my days."

"I have no intention of going anywhere."

"The entire household has been asking of you. It's been quite somber without you and Salvatore about."

"Where has Salvatore been?"

Charlotte patted the chair she now sat in. "Right here. I have taken over playing nursemaid for him several times, only because I could not bear to see him so exhausted. He fought me every time, too, but finally last night when I came in to find him slumped over in the chair, he took up my offer to watch over you, so he could rest for a bit."

"You are a good friend."

Charlotte leaned forward. "And as a dear friend, I must let you know about something."

Nicolette's stomach turned.

"Lady Wellesley asked me about you. She said that her husband believes you to be his child."

Nicolette frowned, uncertain she had heard Charlotte correctly. "He told her about me?"

Charlotte nodded. "It does not take a genius to know the two of you share a remarkable resemblance. You have his eyes, Nic, and the same dimples."

Her father had dimples? She had not noticed. "I have no father, Charlotte."

Pulling the chair closer to the bed, Charlotte took hold of Nicolette's hand. "Simon Laurent has no heir, Nicolette. He and Henrietta have been unable to have children, and he has always yearned for a child. In all truthfulness, can you tell me that the idea of having your father in your life is intolerable?"

"He left my mother pregnant and alone. He did not want me, and he did not want her. When he left her, she was devastated, and I was left to pick up the pieces. I thank God that my mother and I ended up at a brothel where Salvatore and his mother lived. Salvatore is the one who raised me, and my father has him to thank for it. Simon Laurent means nothing to me, nor will he ever. He destroyed my mother, the only family I had left."

"You had Salvatore."

Nicolette nodded. "Yes, I had Salvatore."

"And had Simon not left your mother, you would have never met Salvatore."

"That is true."

"See, fate is a strange thing, is it not?"

Confused by the analogy, Nicolette squeezed her friend's hand in reassurance. "Indeed, it is."

"Will you consider speaking with him?" Charlotte asked, wincing as she did.

Her heart skipped a beat. "He has asked you to speak to me in his stead?"

She nodded. "Indeed, he did. Forgive me, Nic, if I have overstepped the boundaries of our friendship."

"I am not ready to face him yet, but thank you for your honesty."

Nicolette's eyes felt heavy, and she closed them for a moment.

"I have kept you overlong," Charlotte said, standing, and placing a kiss on Nicolette's forehead. "Sleep now, my dear."

Nicolette allowed her friend to tuck her in, and with a promise to be back later, she shut the door behind her.

* * * * *

Salvatore tried to focus on the notes before him, but could not for the life of him finish the score. His mind was a jumble of thoughts and concerns—at the forefront of those concerns was Nicolette.

What kind of person was he, that he had enlisted his best friend, and the love of his life, to seduce his brother? And for what? Revenge? Revenge for what? For their father's neglect, something that Darian Tremayne had no control over?

He would have allowed Nicolette to give her virginity— her truest gift—to the one man he'd despised so much.

It seemed so trivial now. Everything seemed trivial, and with each day that he remained in the house, he was reminded of the sordid plan to bring his brother to ruin, by using his best friend—his beloved—to seek revenge on a man not worthy of the trouble.

Dipping the pen in the ink, he took a deep breath, and hummed the line that had been playing in his head, over and over again. He wrote furiously, the notes dotting the page. The dinner hour came and went. The tray the servant had brought in remained untouched.

And the memories of the past few days, the emotions, tumbled from him onto the page, bringing him the only peace he would know in this despised house.

How fitting that he had almost lost what was most dear, at the very home he had coveted his entire life. It was as though God was telling him that what was important were the people around him, and not the things one had.

Humming the last few notes, he dotted them on the page, and looked down at the parchment with a sense of satisfaction.

The song had poured from him, demanding release. It missed one thing however—a title. He dipped the pen in the ink, and wrote at the top of the page *Nicolette.* With a smile he dotted the I.

A light knock sounded at the door. Earlier he had told the servant to go away, and feeling more than a little guilty, Salvatore walked to the door. He opened it, ready with an apology, to find Simon Laurent standing before him.

"May I have a word with you?" the marquess asked, glancing past Salvatore's shoulder as though he expected someone else to be there.

Salvatore motioned the older man in.

"I hope I am not keeping you from anything." Simon glanced at the sheet of music, and Salvatore shook his head.

"I only just finished." He motioned to a chair. "Please, have a seat."

Simon took the seat closest at hand, and Salvatore sat, wiping his ink-stained hands on a towel.

"You've been writing."

Salvatore nodded, tossed the towel aside. "What can I do for you?"

Clearing his throat, Simon sat back in his chair and steepled his hands together. "I know who you are. I remember you as a child."

A sense of foreboding came over Salvatore, and he quelled the rush of fear that came rising to the surface. "And I remember you."

"You have the eyes of your father," Simon said, brushing an imaginary string from his pants. "Just as Darian does."

So it was out, and Salvatore felt relieved. Almost.

Simon brows furrowed. "I do not pretend to know what my daughter's life was like once I left. Nicolette's mother told me she was pregnant, but I heard rumors that she had other lovers, and in years to come, when I could not sire a child with my wife, I came to the conclusion that Nicolette could not possibly be mine. When I saw her the other day, I felt taken back in time. She resembles her mother so very much, of course, except for her eyes, which—"

"Are yours," Salvatore finished for him.

"Yes, indeed. Just like mine." Simon pursed his lips together. "I have heard you have been instrumental in her life, and for that I owe you a deep gratitude."

"You owe me nothing."

Simon lifted a brow. "I have also heard you are a proud man, and I respect you for that."

Salvatore leaned forward in his chair. "Let us put aside these niceties and get to the real reason you are here."

Simon laughed under his breath, yet the humor did not seem to touch his eyes. "You saved my daughter's life, and I will always be grateful to you for that. Your heroics have been told the past two nights in great detail. You took care of her then, just as you always have, but I am here to set you free of your obligation."

The hairs on the back of Salvatore's neck stood on end. He dreaded the words to come. He shifted in his chair. "I do not understand."

Simon reached into his waistcoat pocket and produced a note. He leaned forward, ready to hand it to Salvatore. "You have taken care of my daughter for long enough. It is now time for me to do my duty by her."

"And you seek to pay me off, and expect me to disappear from her life?" Salvatore controlled his voice, though it took great effort.

Color crept into the marquess cheeks. "I will introduce her to society. She will have a sizeable dowry, and marry well. She will want for nothing."

The icy fingers of dread wrapped around Salvatore's heart.

"I will not be bought, my lord." He ripped the note from Simon's hands and tore it to shreds. "I have loved her, and raised her, and you were not there…and yet you have the gall to sit before me, hand me a note, and think that I will disappear," he snapped his fingers, "just like that?"

"I mean you no disrespect, Salvatore. You yourself would never have to work again. Name your price. I have the ability to give you anything."

Salvatore took an unsteady breath. He only wanted one thing…and that was Nicolette.

"She has lived a life that is not conducive to a debutante. She needs to behave as a young woman of good upbringing. She can not travel about the world without a chaperone, living with a man to whom she is not married."

"I will marry her then."

Simon frowned. "Salvatore, what do you have to offer her?" He looked about the room. "You travel from place to place, staying with members of the aristocracy. In essence, singing for your supper. I ask what will you do when you are no longer the toast of London or Paris? What will you do when someone else comes along to take your place, as all entertainers are replaced. I say this not to hurt you, but to give you a chance at a life you deserve. I know the anger you have for your father. The hurt of being denied a father's love is not something one gets over. Nicolette knows that hurt as well, and I am offering her what even you, Salvatore, cannot give her — the chance to have her father, and to be recognized as my daughter. The possibilities for her will be limitless."

No! The word screamed over and over in his mind, and yet he knew what Simon said was the truth. What could he give her? In time their popularity would fade, and then what? He could teach music, as could she, but would life in a small cottage be enough? They had tasted what wealth and prestige could give. Could one be happy without it? One day they would have to find out. Yet Nicolette had an escape. She *could* live that life…forever. That chance was now staring him in the face.

"You brought her here to seduce your brother, Salvatore. I know that. The countess knows that. She has even asked me about you." Simon laughed without mirth. "She tells me there is something about you that makes her uneasy, and I did not have the heart to tell her that you are her husband's bastard child. That the only reason you came here was to see the marriage between Darian and Elizabeth not take place." Simon bent over and scooped up the pieces of the note and placed them in his pocket. "I know, as do you, the state of Kedgwick's finances. Release her, Salvatore. Give her a chance at the life that you were denied. I will draw up another note, one for considerably more money, and we will no longer speak of the matter. I wish you good luck with your life, young man."

"Nicolette will not hear of it," Salvatore said, coming to his feet, desperate. "She will choose me."

"Nicolette need not know about our arrangement. I know she feels indebted to you, but will you hold that over her head and forego the chance of her having a life she has only dreamed of?" Simon shook his head. "I think not, young man. I think you love her too much to deny her her birthright."

Running a hand through his hair, Salvatore shook his head in disbelief. "You expect me to leave without saying a word to her?"

"I think it best. I know you have a close bond, one that I envy, to be quite honest. Darian has already been told about your scheme, and about your relation to him. He is furious and I've had to restrain him from calling you out. If he has his way, he will see you ruined. The only thing that keeps you here now is my intervention, and the love and loyalty my daughter feels for you."

Salvatore did not even want to know how Darian had reacted to such news. In fact, he did not care about anything. His heart ached too much.

"I have already informed my valet and he will see to your bags. A carriage is awaiting you as we speak." Simon clapped him on the back, and Salvatore flinched. "I give you my word that Nicolette will be safe. I will do her no harm, but will spend the rest of my life making up for the past."

Salvatore could not even move. He stared at Simon as he made his way to the door. The older man opened it, then stopped. "I am forever in your debt, Salvatore. If ever you need anything—anything at all, write to me…and I will see it done, but you are never to see my daughter again."

The marquess closed the door, and Salvatore fell to his knees.

Chapter Fourteen

Єᴏ

Nicolette's appearance at dinner was met by a roaring round of applause. Feeling silly, and with cheeks burning, she made her way to the dinner table, while thanking those who gushed over her.

It seemed ridiculous to be the center of attention for almost getting oneself killed. She would as soon forget the entire matter, but her dinner guests were not about to let her. Tonight she sat with Darian to her right, and Simon Laurent to her left.

Her father pulled out her chair and she managed a smile for him. She did not know what to make of him, and his sudden interest in her life. She had learned to be wary of everyone, particularly men, from a very early age. Perhaps she had grown even more cynical with time.

She looked down the table, hoping to see Salvatore. He had not come back to her room this afternoon as promised, which was so out of character she'd been on edge since waking. Not seeing him amongst the now-familiar faces made her more than a little uneasy. Perhaps he slept? Lord knows he needed the rest. He had looked exhausted earlier.

Deciding that's exactly where he was, she sat back and steadied herself to have her father as her dinner companion. She caught his wife's eye, who sat diagonally across from her, talking to Lord Athenry, who seemed well into his cups already, if Henrietta's pained expression were to tell.

"You look beautiful, my dear," Simon said, a warm smile on his face.

She glanced his way. "Thank you, my lord."

He winced, and she wondered if it was because of her formality. Certainly he did not think she would be so intimate as to call him Father.

That would never happen.

Henrietta smiled warmly. "We are so relieved to see you up and about. What a horrible accident."

"Thank you, Lady Wellesley."

The woman seemed genuine, and for that reason Nicolette felt a wave of guilt. Her mother would roll over in her grave if she knew her daughter actually was growing to like the very woman who had stolen the love of her life away.

Nicolette took a sip of tea and nearly choked on it as a hand stroked the side of her thigh.

Darian smiled at his fiancée who watched him from down the table. The poor dear. She had no idea her betrothed was such a cad and even now, while smiling at her, he groped another.

Trying her best to ignore the roving hand, Nicolette pretended indifference and wished Salvatore would appear. And then a horrible thought came to her. The day of her drowning Darian was supposed to come to her. Now that she had recovered, would he show up tonight? All of the guests would leave tomorrow, including her, which meant Darian would surely take the window of opportunity and make good on his promise to bed her.

She nodded toward the footman across the room. He rushed forward and poured a dollop of wine.

"To the rim please," she said, and Darian laughed under his breath beside her.

"That's the spirit."

She did not even glance in Simon's direction. No doubt he would frown upon her drinking.

Henrietta managed a tight smile and looked to her husband.

Nicolette lifted her glass, and almost dropped it when at her side, Simon tapped on his glass with a fork.

Silence filled the room as Simon stood.

"I'd like to make a toast. To my daughter, the Lady Nicolette Laurent, the most talent pianist in all of Europe."

Gasps followed the declaration, and Nicolette could feel the blood drain from her face as she met Charlotte's shocked smile.

"To Lady Nicolette!" Darian said, standing, pulling Nicolette up to join the others.

The guests raised their cups in toast. "To Lady Nicolette!"

The night had a surreal quality that even hours later did not dissipate. She still could not believe that Simon Laurent had announced her as his daughter in public. Henrietta had tears of joy in her eyes as she hugged Nicolette to her and welcomed her to their family. "I want to be a mother to you," the marchioness had said, and she seemed genuine. Having been denied a mother's love, Nicolette had to admit the thought was tempting.

For all the excitement, there was something missing, and that something, or rather, someone, was Salvatore. If only he had been there to witness the announcement.

"Have you seen Salvatore?" she asked Charlotte while they were having tea with the other women in the drawing room.

Charlotte took a sip of her tea. "No, my dear. I have not, though I did miss his company tonight. He always seems to liven up the conversation. And he is awfully nice to look at."

Nicolette smiled. "Indeed, he is."

"He puts most men to shame, save for one."

Nicolette knew Charlotte meant Darian.

As though sensing they were talking of her beau, Elizabeth took a seat nearby. "I must confess that Lord

Wellesley's declaration came as quite a surprise. I am still reeling from the news."

How odd that in the space of a few hours she had gone from being looked down upon, to being accepted. "As am I," Nicolette said, setting her tea down.

"You and I will be fast friends," Elizabeth said, smiling prettily. "Perhaps you will marry a peer of the crown, and when our husbands are in Parliament, we can throw tea parties and visit the wonderful museums and galleries."

Nicolette did not have the heart to tell Elizabeth that she should not waste her time hoping for something that would never happen. She would never marry a peer of the realm, and she had no inclination to stop playing music. "Perhaps."

Charlotte used her gloved hand to brush away the powdered sugar that had fallen onto her skirts. "Elizabeth, tell me, where will you and Darian honeymoon?"

The woman's cheeks turned bright red. "I would so love to visit New York, though Darian has told my mother that he believes a trip to Greece would do much for his disposition. It seems he is quite tired of the poor weather, and New York is not much better."

"Salvatore and I rent a villa in Greece. A wonderful two-room home with dirt floors and sparse walls. The warm breeze flows in through the open windows, luring one to the gorgeous blue waters below."

Elizabeth sighed. "How fortunate you are, that you have seen so much in your short life."

"Indeed, I am lucky. I'm even more fortunate since I was able to experience it with a dear friend."

Charlotte patted her hand. "Well, you will have to take me to Greece one of these days. I would love to experience it as you have."

Nicolette nodded. "I'd like that, too."

Elizabeth glanced over at Henrietta. "You are so fortunate that Lady Wellesley has accepted you. Can you imagine learning that your husband has a child from another woman?"

"It must have been difficult for her," Nicolette said, meaning it.

"Well, I'm certain if she had her own children, she would not be so forgiving," Elizabeth said, reaching for a strawberry tart. "I doubt I would."

"Oh, I don't know. Some women are good at heart," Charlotte said.

"Why did you not have children?" Elizabeth asked, biting into the tart, and getting crumbs all over her lap.

Charlotte shrugged. "My husband, bless his heart, already had children from his first marriage. He had no desire to have any more. He enjoyed traveling too much, and I never really cared to have children. I like my independence far too much. Yet, I suppose if the right man were to come along, I could easily change my mind."

"And what about you?" Nicolette asked Elizabeth.

Elizabeth choked on the tart. She sat it down, took a sip of tea before responding, "I would like oodles of children. Being an only child is a lonely existence. How I envied my friends who had sisters to play with."

"I've no doubt Darian would be a good father," Charlotte said matter-of-factly, setting the pastry down virtually untouched. Nicolette did not have to wonder what had caused the sudden loss of appetite.

The countess stood and cleared her throat. "Ladies, let us adjourn to the parlor where I have a surprise waiting for all of you."

Charlotte took Nicolette by the hand, and they followed behind Elizabeth who took her mother's hand. They entered the parlor, where at the end of the room a large stage had been set. The women took their seats and the men quickly joined them. The large velvet curtain opened and a portly woman stood, dressed in Napoleon garb.

The guests roared, all but Nicolette, who wished she had been smart like Salvatore and slept through a comedy about the cocky French emperor. Her uneasiness continued as throughout the duration of the play, Nicolette could feel Darian watching her. She did not dare return his gaze, and kept her attention focused on the stage and the ridiculous play.

When at last the curtains closed, and the countess stood and announced Elizabeth would be playing the harp for them, Nicolette decided it was high time to bow out gracefully. She leaned toward Charlotte. "I am quite tired. I think I shall call it a night."

Charlotte nodded. "You have done well hanging in this long. Would you like me to escort you?"

"No, I would not want you to miss Elizabeth's performance."

Charlotte rolled her eyes. "Thank you for abandoning me," she teased.

Nicolette squeezed her friend's hand and made her way to the door, not making eye contact with anyone. She had made it to the hallway when someone grabbed her from behind.

Dread filled her. "Where are you off to?"

It was Darian, a charming smile on his face.

"I fear I'm tired."

"Come, Nicolette. It is your final night here. Stay."

She shook her head. "I'm sorry. I am still so tired."

The chords of the harp called out from the drawing room. "You should return to hear Elizabeth."

"I don't want to. I want to be with you." He reached out, and cupped her chin in his hand. "You are refusing me again."

It wasn't a question.

"I do not refuse you."

His eyes lit up. "Then you will be waiting for me?"

She nodded. "Of course, my lord. I believe a warm bath and a chilled glass of wine will do me wonders."

"You already drank a glass, Nicolette. Do you wish to be intoxicated?"

"Of course not. Though I confess to being nervous."

He took her hand, and putting his fingers to his lips, signaled silence as he pulled her into the library and shut the door.

"You make me crazy with wanting."

The room was pitch-black. With her back flat against the wall, she felt at a definite disadvantage. It took great control not to push against him and race for her room.

"If only Simon had declared you his daughter before I became engaged to Elizabeth."

Her heart skittered.

"Then how I would yearn for my wedding day. As it is…now I cringe when I think of the noose that is to be my marriage."

"Surely it will not be that bad."

"I do not want her."

"Family honor is a double-edged sword at times."

"Indeed," Darian replied, palming her face in his hands.

"I have no wish to marry. I want only to have you. I almost wish that you were not Simon's daughter. How I yearn to have you as my lady."

Not his lady—but his mistress. For the first time, Nicolette was relieved to be the daughter of a marquess.

* * * * *

Salvatore watched the passing landscape.

Simon Laurent had wasted no time in seeing his bags packed and Salvatore escorted to the awaiting carriage.

Simon had stood, hands clasped behind his back, watching until the carriage pulled out of the drive. The marquess had stuffed the note in Salvatore's jacket pocket, and though it had been hours, he still could not bear to look at it.

He was being paid to stay away from the person he held most dear.

He shook with fury. Even now, his anger did not ebb, but instead grew stronger. He had not even been allowed to see Nicolette one last time. How he had yearned to open the door, to see her smile just once.

God, how would he live without her?

The lights of London flickered in the distance, and Salvatore sat up straight. His future seemed so uncertain, and he didn't even know where to go. He would need to cancel their engagements, though perhaps the proprietors would allow a solo act?

He could not stay at their hotel, for that is where Nicolette would look for him, and he did not think he could bear to see her now. She had another life to live, and he would not be part of it.

And in an instant he knew where he would go.

He leaned out of the carriage and yelled to the driver, "To Drury Lane."

Chapter Fifteen

ഇ

Nicolette knocked on Salvatore's door. When she received no answer, she opened it to find the room dark and empty. Further investigation showed he had not slept in the bed at all.

"May I help you?" a passing maid asked, startling Nicolette.

"Have you seen the gentleman who's been staying in this room?"

The maid shook her head. "No, my lady. I have not."

With a curt nod, she left Nicolette alone. Perhaps he was in her room? Hope quickened her steps, but she was bitterly disappointed to find the room empty.

Where in the world could he be? Her mind raced. She stepped onto the balcony and looked over the lawns, but could see no one, save Mrs. Stromme who puffed on a cigar.

Shutting the balcony doors behind her, Nicolette walked toward the door when it opened.

She held her breath, and let it out a moment later when Darian stepped in, a wicked smile on his face. How exhausting he was!

Nicolette's pulse skittered as he made quick work of his cravat. "I thought I would join you in that bath."

She swallowed hard. "I did not call for one yet."

"Oh, but I did." He stopped to pull his boots off.

Oh God! She could not find Salvatore and Darian apparently was quite determined. What could she say? What could she do to stop what was going to happen to indeed happen?

A tap sounded at the door. Darian rushed back and opened it. His valet entered, and with five footmen behind him carrying buckets, they began the long process of filling the tub.

Once the men left, Darian strode toward her and lifted her in his arms. "You are mine tonight. No one will interrupt us."

"What of your mother or Elizabeth?"

He put a finger to her lips. "Do not worry, my sweet. I have it all arranged. The servants have been paid well for their silence, I assure you."

Again, a tap at the door, and once again a steady stream of footman appeared with their steaming buckets.

Embarrassed, Nicolette went to the window and looked out. *Salvatore, where are you?* When the door closed, Darian locked it, then made quick work of his shirt.

His pants followed until he stood in just his drawers, holding his arms out to her.

Sweet Jesus, how would she get out of this?

"I cannot make love to you!" she blurted, pushing aside the fear that quickly rose to the surface.

He looked amused. "What do you mean? Of course you can. Now, come here." He motioned for her to come to him.

Her legs were as heavy as lead, and she found she could not move. "I can not."

Irritation showed on his face. "Then I shall come to you." He took the steps that separated them.

There was nowhere to go, nowhere to hide. "Wait!"

He frowned while running a hand through his hair. "I do not understand what game you play, Nicolette, but it is not wise to push a man so far!"

She did not like the expression on his face. In fact, she actually feared him in that moment, and felt the urgent need to escape. But he was too fast. He caught her in his arms, squeezing her tight to him. "You little vixen. I do not understand the games you play, but I am most willing to play along—but only as long as in the end I have you beneath me."

An image of his body bowing over hers made her wince. She did not want to make love to anyone but Salvatore.

"It is not that I don't want you. I do, but I am so terribly worried about Salvatore."

Darian's fingers tightened on her arms. "Salvatore is fine."

Her heart leapt. "Where is he?"

He frowned. "You do not know?"

Foreboding washed over her in waves. "What do you mean?"

Darian lifted his brows. "I thought your father would have told you."

"Darian, please, tell me what you're talking about. Where is Salvatore?"

"Salvatore has left Kedgwick Manor."

Her pulse skittered with alarm. She could not believe it. Salvatore had left...without saying anything to her. "That is preposterous. He would never leave me? H...how long ago did he leave?"

"This afternoon."

"What did you do to him?"

Darian looked like she'd slapped him. "I did nothing to the man, though God knows I should have."

"What is that supposed to mean?"

The side of Darian's lips curved in an eerie smile. "I know who Salvatore is, Nicolette. I also understand he came here hoping for revenge...a revenge that could have easily happened, had my friend Simon Laurent not arrived. Imagine my shock and surprise when Simon told me who Salvatore truly was. I knew my father sired bastards all over the continent, but little did I know one would come seeking vengeance. I have to hand it to him—the boy is smart. He knew I could not resist you."

Darian pulled her close, until their lips were inches apart. "I will have you, Nicolette. I do not care if you are the daughter of my friend, or even if the duke finds out I've cuckolded his daughter. I have been denied for far too long, and you have played the game far too well. What harm will a little pleasure do us?"

"I need to go to Salvatore."

He pushed her from him so abruptly, she fell and landed on her bottom.

His cheeks reddened but he made no move to help her up. "He does not want you any longer. In fact, he seemed relieved that Simon offered to take you off his hands."

She scrambled to her feet. "You lie!"

"Salvatore would not leave you…until Simon offered him money." Darian took a step closer and lifted the curl that had rested above her bosom. "I must say, he took the offer and ran with it. Simon said he barely stopped to pack his bags."

Nicolette reeled with the news. Salvatore had been paid off? No, it was unthinkable. He would *never* take money. He loved her.

Or did he?

Perhaps the money had been a godsend, and why else would he not have stopped to say goodbye? He had not even written her a letter.

Fury and pain raced through her.

"I understand it pains you to know he took the money and ran, but know this much. I can be your protector now. I will give you anything you desire. You need not worry about money, clothes, a home. Name your price—I will give you anything."

"What would my father think of your offer, I wonder?"

Darian lifted a brow. "Come, Nicolette. You may be the newly acknowledged daughter of a peer of the realm, but you are still a bastard. Even Simon knows that you may be accepted by society, but you will never truly be a blue blood."

The words were a sharp slap to the face, and they gave her the courage she needed most desperately to rush past him, toward the door.

She struggled with the key, and in an instant Darian was behind her, his hard body pressed against her, pushing her against the door, his manhood like stone against her back.

The key fell from her fingers.

"You will not leave, Nicolette."

"Darian, let me go."

"I will not," he said, lifting her skirts with his hands.

Panic ensued, and Nicolette smacked her hand against the door. "Hel…"

Darian clamped a hand over her mouth and she bit him. "Little witch," he said, trying again, clamping his hand so tight against her lips she tasted blood.

He lifted her skirts about her waist, and she could feel the hard length of him against her buttocks. She tried to wrench away, but he pushed her harder against the door, her cheek pressed against the hard wood.

The more she moved, it seemed the more excited he became. She pounded on the door again.

"Nicolette?"

It sounded like Elizabeth.

Darian went still behind her, and her skirts fell to the floor once again. Relief washed over her in waves. "Answer her," Darian whispered against her ear, loosening his grip.

"Yes?"

"Open the door, Nicolette," This time it was Charlotte's voice.

"Do not open it," Darian whispered.

"Just a minute," she called out, and Darian cursed under his breath. An instant later he was rushing about the room, picking up his clothing. He raced over to the balcony, then thinking better of it, and better yet, what he would look like to any guests in the garden, he slid beneath the bed.

Still shaking, Nicolette smoothed out her skirts and then opened the door.

Charlotte stood in front of Elizabeth, her brows furrowed into a frown. Her friend glanced past her shoulder into the room. "What is wrong?"

Nicolette wished Elizabeth were not here. She would tell all if it were just Charlotte. And she needed her friend to talk to, to try to understand what had happened with Salvatore. Tears filled her eyes and she blinked them back. "Nothing."

Charlotte's eyes narrowed. "You were knocking at the door, as though you were in distress."

"Sorry, I was having a difficult time with the lock. I let my temper get the best of me."

Charlotte did not buy it. "Let me try it," she said, stepping into the room. "Elizabeth, dear, why don't you go on to your room? I am sure your mother will be checking on you soon."

The girl looked relieved. "Very well, I shall see you both at breakfast."

Charlotte shut the door behind them. "The truth."

Nicolette nodded toward the bed.

Charlotte lifted a tawny brow, and with a malicious smile she walked toward the bed, taking a seat in one of the chairs. "So, what are you up to?"

"I am getting ready to leave."

"What?" This came from beneath the bed, a moment before Darian slid out, his pants on but unbuttoned.

Charlotte's mouth gaped open, clearly surprised by Darian's state of undress. "What in God's name are you up to now, Kedgwick? Your mother will have your head if she finds you in here. She looked for you earlier during Elizabeth's pitiful performance. I do not have to wonder where you were…since I did not see Nicolette either. I was on my way here when Elizabeth rushed behind me."

Nicolette did not have time to be reprimanded. She only had one thought in mind and that was to get to London posthaste. Rushing past the widow and Darian, she pulled her clothing from drawers and the wardrobe, tossing them on the bed.

"Nicolette, what in God's name," Charlotte inquired.

"I must leave. Now."

"You will not leave at night. It is not safe," Darian said, agitation filling his voice.

"I will chance it," Nicolette replied, reaching for her valise. She grabbed hold of the bell pull and rang.

"For Christ's sake, Nicolette. Will you stop for an instant," Darian said, his tone relaying his fury.

"I do not have time."

"He left you, Nic. He took the money and ran."

He might as well have slapped her. "Salvatore did not take the money. I know him."

"Will someone please tell me what is going on?" Charlotte asked standing, hands on hips.

"Salvatore left this afternoon. Simon paid him to leave me," Nicolette said matter-of-factly.

Darian laughed without mirth. "Salvatore had a choice."

In that moment she had never hated anyone more. "I do not believe you, Darian. Salvatore loves me, I know that."

The nerve in her jaw ticked in double time. "He loved you so much he had you seduce me? He was willing to pimp you in order to get his revenge."

Charlotte gasped.

"He has spent his entire life taking care of you. He is a young man, Nicolette," Darian said, grabbing hold of her wrist. "Allow him the chance to live for once. He has money, he has a career, and he will survive, as you will survive without him."

Nicolette wrenched away from him. Did he speak the truth? Did Salvatore truly leave because he had made a fortune, and wished to be free of her? Did he look at her as a hindrance?

Nicolette blinked back tears. "He loves me."

"He does. I will not deny that." Darian lifted a dark brow. "And if you loved him, you would let him go. Give him the freedom he has never had."

"Oh do shut up, Darian!" Charlotte put her hand on Nicolette's shoulder. "Do not leave tonight. I understand your haste, but the roads are not safe. You could be set upon by thieves, and lord knows who else."

She was right. Nicolette knew it. She glanced at Darian. "You need to go."

Darian quirked his lips.

Charlotte turned to him and motioned him out of the room.

When the door shut behind him, Nicolette finally allowed herself to weep.

Chapter Sixteen

Though Simon Laurent had given his word that he would do everything in his power to keep Darian from destroying him, Salvatore was fast realizing that his brother had the power to destroy him, with or without the marquess help.

Already he could feel the chill when entering a reception hall after playing. Those who had been kind, now held their chins higher, smiled tightly, turned their back to him. Even the applause came less often.

He had known it would all end one day, but he had just not expected it to be so soon…and not because of his brother.

Perhaps he would go to Paris and visit his old friend Count de Vassey. Yet every time he thought of the kindly old man, he thought of Nicolette. How happy they had been there. There was always Greece, but that would be even worse, since Nicolette loved the villa so much. Every city seemed to have a memory attached to the one woman he could not get out of his mind.

A knock sounded at his door. He pulled on a shirt, and answered it to find Nalise, a pretty Irish girl with red hair and forest green eyes. Standing there she reminded him of Nicolette in so many ways.

The night he had returned to the brothel he had met her. Only fifteen, and an orphan, Nalise had found it easier to sell her body, than work as a governess, or servant to a man who would use her any way he pleased.

Wearing a gaudy black satin gown, she smiled prettily. "What a' ya' doin', Salvatore," she asked, biting into her rouged lower lip.

"I am preparing for tonight's concert."

She played with the ribbon that held her bodice together. "Where da ya' play?"

"At Baron Cardowis' anniversary celebration, and I have been asked to play two sets."

"Would ya' like a little tumble before ya' go. I won't charge ya' or nothin'."

He had not bedded anyone since Nicolette, and though his body yearned for release, he could not. "Not tonight, Nalise."

She pouted. "Please." Her gaze shifted from his, down his chest, and lower still. "I can make ya' happy."

"I'm sure you could. But I am late as it is."

"Tonight then?"

He would have to leave here. He knew that now. In fact, he had stayed far too long as it was. "Perhaps," he said, having no such inclination.

"Okay." She went up on the tips of her toes and kissed him on the lips.

She walked away, her hips swaying enticingly.

Salvatore shut the door behind her. Perhaps he should give into his desires? Maybe then he could forget about Nicolette, forget the feelings she had fired within him.

God help him but he could not even leave the city in the hopes of running into her again.

He had heard she was in town, staying with Charlotte. There had been many a time when he'd driven past her house, looking out the carriage window, hoping to catch a mere glimpse.

How did she fare, he wondered.

Did she miss him even a little?

* * * * *

"You are melancholy again."

Nicolette glanced up from where she sat at the piano and forced a smile. Charlotte had been kind enough to invite her to stay at her London townhouse, and for the past two months the widow had made it her mission to keep her mind off Salvatore, an almost impossible task.

Having left Kedgwick Hall, Nicolette had gone straight to the hotel where they'd been staying since arriving in London. To her great regret Salvatore was not there. She had gone to every venue in town, asked everyone they had worked for in the past if they had seen him. The answer was the same. No one had seen him.

It was as though he had disappeared from the face of the Earth. No letter, no warning, just gone.

For two months she had waited for word, spending endless days, taking refuge in her writing, pouring her heart into the notes. Salvatore would be proud of her progress. She practiced more now than she ever did, but she did so now for a different reason. Music was her saving grace, her passion, and if she did not have it, she feared she would die from the pain.

She settled her hand over her stomach. She had not had her menses for two months, and though she was not sick in the mornings, she was almost certain she carried Salvatore's child. She did not dare tell another soul, not even Charlotte, her constant companion.

A footman walked in with a silver tray bearing calling cards and letters. Charlotte set aside her needlepoint, and one by one went through the correspondence.

"There are several letters for you. One from your father and Henrietta. They've returned from Italy." Charlotte released a sigh. "And Darian is at it again. Will the man never give up?"

Darian's letters had gone unread. Many times she just tossed them in the fire. Charlotte would watch, her brows furrowed, but she remained silent.

Nicolette ran her fingers over the keys again. Her father had made it a point to include her in his life. He wanted her to move into his London townhouse, but Nicolette would not have it. Salvatore would have never left her had it not been for Simon Laurent. Her father once again had ruined everything. True, she was being recognized from all those who had snubbed her before, but she had never coveted their acceptance to begin with.

"Oh my goodness!" Charlotte exclaimed, coming to her feet. "We have been invited to Lord Cardowis' anniversary party — and it is tonight."

Nicolette cringed. She had no desire to go to a ball. She had attended two so far, and every time she had danced, conversed and then come home sadder than before. It was the first time she had been without Salvatore, and every dance partner she compared to him. She did not want their attention. She wanted only to have the life she'd once led— traveling, playing...being with Salvatore.

She hated what her life had become. Women coming to call, to have tea and speak of trivial things such as the weather, and gossip about things Nicolette did not care about. The men were even more tedious then the women. She didn't like being thought of as a prized mare. From the moment she and Charlotte entered a room, she could feel the eyes of the men on her, the women gossiping behind her back. Many times she heard Darian's name attached to hers.

Thank goodness he had been out of the country.

Charlotte bit into her lower lip. "Darian is back in town. He shall be there tonight! Oh, as will your father!"

Nicolette did not have the heart to tell Charlotte that now she was even less inclined to go. Though she did enjoy conversing with her father and Henrietta, Darian was a completely different matter.

"Come, we have so much to do. I think you should wear the new gown we bought at Madame le Broe's last week. I have a string of pearls that will look beautiful woven through your hair." Charlotte clapped her hands together. "Oh, what fun it shall be."

Nicolette could do nothing but follow her excited friend up the stairs to their respective bedchambers. She did not want to ruin Charlotte's excitement. It was most unfortunate that the widow had fallen in love with Darian Tremayne. The man did not deserve a woman like her. She was too good for the rakehell earl.

* * * * *

Nicolette had been at the ball for hours, dancing every once in awhile, but for the most part trying to stay as far away from Darian Tremayne as humanly possible.

The earl, with his mother on his arm, had entered the cavernous room, and stopped at the top of the stairs while the footman called out his name. Nicolette counted to thirty before the man proceeded down the stairway, his gaze scouring the crowd, which became all atwitter at his arrival.

She had tried to disappear in the crowd, stepping behind the portly Viscount Ladley for a time, but as a sheep could not hide from the wolf for overlong, so she could not hide from Darian.

Dressed in formal black, as many of the other men, he had reached for her hand and brought it to his lips. "Nicolette, you have only grown more beautiful with time." He turned to Charlotte. "Hello Char, how are you?"

Charlotte lifted her hand, and Darian obediently took it and quickly kissed it. He instantly turned his attention back to Nicolette, and she instantly noted her friend's disappointment. "May I get you some punch?"

"That would be wonderful, thank you."

"I would like a glass as well," Charlotte chimed in. Darian smiled tightly at his old friend and motioned for a footman to serve them. God forbid he walk to get them the drinks.

Darian's gaze hovered over her cleavage. Her breasts had grown these past months, making her gowns fit tighter in the bodice than before. Tonight she felt downright obscene, and it didn't help that Darian all but drooled. He leaned forward and whispered in her ear, "You tease me mercilessly, Nicolette. Already I want you in my bed."

Merciful heavens, were they back to that again?

She managed a weak smile, which disappeared a moment later when her father and Henrietta were introduced. Everyone went silent, and more than a few looked in her direction.

Darian, taking Nicolette by the hand, parted the crowd like the Red Sea and walked through, giving Simon a hearty clap on the back.

"Nicolette, my darling, how are you?" Henrietta asked, embracing her. Others watched the scene play out, and Nicolette hugged her stepmother, and kissed her cheek. She adored Henrietta, and she would not give anyone room for speculation.

Her father stepped forward and brought her hand to his lips. "You have grown even more beautiful these past two months. I daresay Charlotte has worked wonders. It looks like you have put on a stone."

The reference to her weight gain made Nicolette more than a bit embarrassed. She just hoped no one would guess what had caused it. "I feel very good," she replied, glancing over her shoulder, hoping to find Charlotte heading their way, but the widow was no longer there.

"I have a surprise for you this evening, my dear," Simon said, extending his arm. She wrapped her hand in the crook of his arm, leaving Henrietta and Darian to converse. "But first let us dance."

Nicolette had always loved to dance, and it seemed odd to be doing so with her father, a man she had never dreamed to have a relationship with. He was quite light on his feet, and she had to admit that she liked the way he smiled at her, with such open adoration and approval. She could hear others talk, and she realized in that moment that despite him sending Salvatore away, she was happy to have him in her life. She had not realized how much she had come to depend on Salvatore in that role.

The song ended, and went right into a waltz, a dance that was still relatively new, and looked down upon by some. It appeared that the host did not have such qualms as he stepped out on the floor, pulling his wife to him.

"May I?" Simon asked, and Nicolette placed her hands in his, remembering too well the last time she had danced the waltz. It had been with Salvatore. They had danced so scandalously close, that others had whispered behind their hands, and she had loved shocking them all.

Suddenly a shadow fell over them. "May I have this dance?" Darian asked, a wolfish smile on his face.

"Of course you may," Simon responded, handing her over to Darian without a second glance.

Darian was not as light on his feet as her father, nor did he hold her at such a respectable distance. Nicolette braced her arms against him. "You are the most beautiful woman here."

"Thank you," she murmured, noting the group of women watching them, many behind fans.

"Is Elizabeth here?"

"No, did you not hear?" He laughed wickedly. "We are no longer betrothed."

Now that was shocking. "Truly?"

"Indeed." He smiled down at her, obviously of no mind to tell all.

"What happened?"

"I realized that I was marrying the wrong woman."

Her stomach rolled. She did not want to ask the next question, and it seemed she didn't have to since he added, "You are the woman I want, Nicolette."

"I do not wish to marry."

His lips quirked. "*All* women wish to marry, Nicolette, and your father has been good enough to accept on your behalf."

How like a man to tell her what she wanted.

"Your mother must be distraught."

He sighed heavily. "For a fortnight or two, but I have assured her I will marry soon, and have lots of children." His gaze shifted to her breasts. "I can hardly wait to get you with child."

Nicolette missed a beat, and nearly tripped over Darian's feet. He steadied her. "Ah, I can see you are most anxious, too."

Thankfully the song ended, and she nodded curtly before departing. Darian grabbed hold of her wrist and pulled her out onto the veranda, which was lit up with multicolored lights. An elderly couple sat on a stone bench and looked up when Nicolette and Darian walked out. They smiled at them, then each other.

"I have missed you horribly," he said, taking her hand in his and kissing it. "I swear, Nicolette. There was not a day that I did not think of you."

She ripped her hand from his. "Stop it!"

"Why did you not respond to my letters?"

She looked up at him, and hated how his eyes reminded her so much of Salvatore's. "I did not have anything to say."

He put his fingers under her chin, lifting the slightest bit. "I have forgiven you."

How very admirable of him. She yearned to slap his hand away, but did not dare. The walls had eyes and ears, and she did not want to shame Simon and Henrietta in any way, particularly since they had been so kind to her.

For all their niceties, she could not help but kick herself for her current predicament. If only she and Salvatore had not come up with the scheme, then she would not be here now.

She opened her mouth to respond when she heard the thrum of a violin coming from the ballroom. The breath lodged in her throat, and she looked to the large windows that lined the ballroom. She could not see past the crowd, and a huge column stood in way of the stage.

Nicolette raced for the ballroom, and made her way through the crowd. Her heart slammed to a stop. Salvatore stood on stage, eyes closed, playing Beethoven's Violin Sonata No. 5 in F major.

Dressed brilliantly in a black suit, snow-white shirt, cravat and a gold waistcoat, his hair was even longer than last she saw him. Her heart pounded in time to the music, her stomach clenching in anticipation. Lord, how she had missed him, and now she drank in the sight.

Charlotte had found her way to Nicolette, and she took hold of her hand, squeezing it tight in her own.

Nicolette could not tear her eyes away as Salvatore played. He seemed in his own world, and she realized with a start, that he had not changed the way he played at all, except for who he played with. A woman dressed in a gold gown that matched the color of Salvatore's waistcoat perfectly, sat at the piano, her fingers dancing over the keys.

Raw jealousy ripped through Nicolette. She could not believe she had so easily been replaced.

The woman watched Salvatore without blinking, her movements mechanical, but not at all fluid. To others she played splendidly, but Nicolette felt she needed immense work, particularly on *Moonlight Serenade*, a song Nicolette and Salvatore had written while in South Africa.

Pushing aside the raw jealousy, Nicolette stared at Salvatore. He was thinner, but healthy, and she wondered if he missed her even a little. Perhaps the money he had acquired made up for the loss of her friendship.

If only she could forget him as he had forgotten her.

Nicolette's throat grew tight. He had written new songs in their time apart, and the notes tugged at her heart.

Lord, how I have missed that sweet sound. She had not realized how much until now.

Song after song he played, his charming smile in place for the crowd, who adored him. Roses were thrown on stage, no doubt women clamoring for his attention. Jealousy raged within Nicolette seeing a beautiful blonde near side stage. In between a song he took the rose from the woman, and kissed her hand.

"She does not hold a candle to you," Charlotte murmured, but it did not help the envy or pain she felt.

When he finished the set, the crowd applauded, but it was fast in coming and quit far too soon. Salvatore, taking his partner by the hand, bowed while the brunette took her curtsy.

Along with the faint applause, she also noted that more than a few people were looking in Darian's direction. Had he told them about Salvatore's plan to ruin him? It seemed word had leaked.

Salvatore, with smile still in place, exited off the stage with his partner in tow.

She looked at Darian and she had her answer. He had not been quiet about the intended seduction. He had told anyone who would listen what Salvatore had done, probably even leaving her out of it...or perhaps saying she was also a victim of Salvatore's scheme. If possible, she hated him even more at that moment.

* * * * *

Salvatore's partner kissed his cheek. "I will be back in quarter of an hour. Is that plenty of time before the next set?"

"Indeed, it is, Marcel. Now, go, your husband will be waiting for you."

The woman, a student of his, had offered to play with him tonight. He knew that the reason for her offer was to attend a ball, especially one as prestigious as Baron Cardowis' ball. Being the daughter of a milliner, she had never seen what the other half lived like, and tonight she had seen the true ugliness of it all. No wonder she was anxious to return to her husband, who waited near the servants' entrance.

"Ladies and gentlemen, may I have your attention please."

The announcement brought Salvatore to the double doors off the grand ballroom. The host of tonight's festivities, Lord Cardowis, stood with a couple on stage. Adrenaline rushed through his veins. It was Simon Laurent and his wife, Henrietta.

The room of four-hundred-plus guests gathered around. His curiosity piqued, Salvatore took a step in, his heart trip-hammering. If Simon Laurent were here, then chances were Nic would be too.

Or would she?

His gaze scanned the crowd, his heart pounding hard every time he saw a woman with auburn hair. Then he spotted Nicolette standing next to Charlotte. Her hair had been swept up in an elegant coiffure that showed her long neck to perfection. A string of pearls had been woven throughout the auburn tresses, matching the ones that encased her slender throat. She was not looking at the stage, but at the crowd, and he had the audacity to wonder, even for a moment, if she searched for him. Obviously she had seen him play.

All night he had felt nervous, and while he played he had not allowed himself the luxury of looking out over the sea of faces. He was sure if he had seen her then, he would not have been able to get through the first set. As it was, it would be most difficult to continue on with the next set.

His heart constricted. She had grown even more beautiful in his absence.

"On this special night that marks my twenty-fifth wedding anniversary, I have the distinct honor of introducing another joining."

Salvatore's palms started to sweat when the baron nodded to Simon, who stepped forward.

Lord Wellesley cleared his throat and held his hand out to Nicolette.

Nicolette glanced at Charlotte, who urged her forward. Looking like she'd rather be anywhere else, she took her father's hand.

The marquess kissed her hand. "This is my daughter Lady Nicolette Laurent."

"Ahh," the crowd said nearly in unison, as though they had not heard the gossip a full two months before. Applause followed the introduction.

"Please join me in welcoming Nicolette into my family."

Simon beamed down at his daughter, kissing her on the cheek, then Henrietta did the same, but went a step further by embracing her, no doubt winning points as being the most understanding wife of *the ton*. Salvatore doubted most women of the peerage would be so accepting of their husband's bastard children.

"I also have the immense pleasure in announcing a most grand event."

The hair on Salvatore's arms stood on end and foreboding washed over him. Walking through the crowd, a head taller than the rest, was Darian Tremayne. He made his way to the stage, a confident smile on his face.

Nicolette shifted on her feet, looking from her father to Darian then back again. He could see she was surprised at the announcement as she stared in disbelief.

Dear God what were they about?

Salvatore pushed away from the wall, having half a mind to stop what was surely about to happen.

A hand clamped over his wrist. It was Viscount Athenry, Darian's friend who'd been at Kedgwick Manor. "I suggest you stay where you are," he said, a tight smile on his face. "You are merely the entertainment here, and don't you forget it."

"And here he is," Simon said, clasping hands with Darian. "It is my great honor to announce the engagement of my daughter, Lady Nicolette, to Darian Tremayne, Earl of Kedgwick."

Salvatore closed his eyes, unable to stand the sight of the man he hated more than life, claiming the woman he loved more than life itself…and lost.

He had no one to blame but himself.

There were gasps and many shocked faces, and then everyone politely applauded.

"I wanted you, my dearest friends, to hear it from me first," Simon said. "Please know that you all will be invited to the upcoming nuptials."

Simon took Henrietta's hand, while Darian took Nicolette's.

Salvatore wrenched away from the viscount's grip. "I have a set to play."

Chapter Seventeen

ဆ

"May I have a word with you?"

Though it had been just a quarter of an hour since the announcement of her engagement, Nicolette had not had a moment to say a single word. She could not have if she wanted to, so shocked and stunned she was by Simon's audacity.

Darian turned to her, a steady smile in place. "Of course."

Aware that eyes followed them everywhere, Nicolette smiled prettily at him. "I have no desire to marry you."

Darian's eyes narrowed. "I thought you would be most anxious to hear the news. You could do far worse than marrying an earl, my dear."

"I think it is incredibly arrogant, not to mention rude of you to announce my engagement to me at the same time you are telling all of London."

The sides of his mouth curved into a cruel smile. "You are the envy of every woman here, Nic."

Nicolette lifted a brow. "That is incredibly arrogant, and please do not call me Nic."

"I will call you what I please." He shrugged.

"They are probably wondering what happened to Elizabeth? Did you once consider her feelings in this matter?"

"No doubt they look at you and know what happened to Elizabeth. Often times upon these turn of events, people tend to think what they want." He let his gaze slip past her lips to her breasts. "In this case they will probably assume that you are already increasing with my child."

Nicolette's cheeks burned. Did he guess her condition, or was it mere coincidence? Is that what everyone would think? Of course it was.

"Nic, it is a bit late for blushes now, isn't it?"

She did not like him calling her Nic. That nickname had been reserved for Salvatore.

"I do not want to marry you."

He lifted a brow. "Do you want Salvatore to be ruined? You know I have the power to bring about his downfall. He planned to do the same to me. I simply was returning the favor."

"I've little doubt you've already set about ruining him." If possible, he had sunk to an even lower level. "Why would you seek to hurt him? He's done nothing to you."

Darian snorted. "He has done enough."

"Like what? You never desired to marry Elizabeth, and now you aren't."

"Indeed, now I will have a beautiful wife, and receive a nice dowry as well."

"Simon is giving you a dowry?"

"Don't you think it time you call me Father?"

Nicolette started at the sound of Simon's voice. He clamped hands with Darian.

"I shall be honored to call you Father," Darian said, going so far as to embrace Simon.

"And I will be honored to call you my son," Simon returned.

Nicolette looked to Henrietta for help, but the woman just smiled, obviously elated by the news.

She would get no help from that quarter, but she knew whom she could depend on.

Charlotte.

"Will you please excuse me for a moment? I need to find someone," Nicolette said, stepping past them, but Darian grabbed her by the shoulder.

"Where are you going, Nicolette?"

Nicolette turned, and prying Darian's hand from her shoulder, replied, "I am going to see Charlotte. I would appreciate it if you would not treat me like your possession."

"Nicolette," Simon said beneath his breath. "You are behaving shamelessly. Darian is your betrothed and he has every right to know where you are off to."

"And I told him where I was going, *Simon*."

Her father's brows furrowed. "You will give me the respect I am due, Nicolette."

Oh, how she yearned to tell him that he did not deserve her respect. What would all these people think if they knew the real Lord Wellesley? A man who had loved an actress, then turned her into a whore because of his abandonment of them. "I am off to see my friend."

Without another word, Nicolette left the three of them watching after her.

Nicolette scoured the room, looking for Salvatore.

Praying he had not left, she spied Charlotte sitting by an elderly woman in the corner. Nicolette made her way toward her friend, when from the corner of her eye she saw Salvatore and his partner walk onstage.

He looked straight at her. No smile, no expression at all.

Her heart hammered so loud, it was a roar that filled her ears.

Salvatore cleared his throat. "I would like to start this set with a song I wrote for a dear friend of mine. I have never played it in public before, so you are the first to hear it."

Darian stepped up beside her, putting a possessive hand around her waist. Nicolette felt it like a cold weight. Salvatore ran the bow over the strings, the tune a lighthearted melody that seemed to express their years as children. While he played, he continued to look straight at her, and people were beginning to notice. Darian stiffened at her side.

As the song continued, it slowed and saddened. Tears burned her eyes and she wondered if that is how he felt now, because it surely was how she had felt since they had parted.

A tear ran down her cheek, onto her chest, only to be followed by another. The music picked up once again, and then he blended the two, almost in a chaotic way, that had the crowd clapping loudly.

It ended on a haunting note. Then and only then, did he break eye contact, nodding his thanks to the crowd. He turned to his partner, who took her seat at the bench, and they played a waltz. Darian took her hand. "Come, dance with me."

"I do not care to."

"Wipe the tears from your eyes, Nicolette."

She frowned. "Why?"

"I will not have my fiancée pining for a violinist." He said the words as though it disgusted him. Like Salvatore was so beneath him.

"He is my friend, and I love him more than anyone else in this world." He squeezed her hand tight and she winced. "My lord, I suggest you let go of me now, or I will scream so loud, it will wake the dead."

She could tell by expression alone that he believed she bluffed. Nicolette opened her mouth and he dropped her hand.

Nicolette found Charlotte still sitting beside the elderly woman. Her friend looked pale, and instantly concerned, she took the seat to her left. "Are you all right?"

Charlotte nodded. "I suppose I should be asking you that question."

There was no condemnation in her voice, just curiosity.

"I am not marrying him, Charlotte. You know that."

Charlotte smiled sadly. "I thought as much. I could see the shock on your face when the announcement was made."

"I did not want to hurt Simon."

"I know you don't. But what of yourself?"

Nicolette glanced at the stage, where Salvatore played. He had his eyes closed.

"He is so gorgeous, Nic." Charlotte sighed. "Look at all the women in the room. Look at how they watch him."

Nicolette had always made such a point to close her eyes while playing, that she had never really noticed how enraptured the audience became. Women and men alike stared—even the ones dancing. Salvatore's beauty was so striking, one could not help but admire him.

"I do not know how you composed yourself when he played you that song. You know it was for you and you alone."

Nicolette nodded. "Yes, I knew, and I scarcely kept my composure."

"I know. I could see you cry." She winked. "I have good news for you."

"What?"

"My friend, Madeline, has invited us to a little get-together over at the Clarendon Hotel, not far from here. I have it on good authority that Salvatore will be there."

Excitement rushed through Nicolette. "But what of Darian? He'll never let me go without him."

Charlotte pursed her lips together. "You just leave Darian to me."

* * * * *

The reception room at the Clarendon Hotel was standing room only. Nicolette smoothed out the skirts of her forest green gown. "How do I look?"

"Perfect, as always," Charlotte murmured. "Look, there he is." Charlotte pointed across the room, to where Salvatore stood talking with an older gentleman. He laughed at something the man said, nodding in agreement.

She had never been so nervous. Her palms were sweating beneath her gloves. Charlotte took charge, taking Nicolette by the hand and making her way directly to Salvatore.

They were intercepted by Madeline, who exclaimed, "You must let me do the honor." Smiling like the cat who ate the canary, she tapped on Salvatore's shoulder.

Salvatore turned, his gaze shifting from Madeline to her.

Nicolette's heart missed a beat.

His smile faltered, but only for a moment. "Nicolette," he said, his eyes shifting over her, searching her face. "You look amazing."

"So do you."

"Why don't we find some punch," Charlotte said to Madeline and the older gentleman, leaving her and Salvatore alone.

She shifted on her feet. "You played wonderfully tonight."

The sides of his mouth lifted, and her stomach tightened. How she had missed that smile. "Thank you."

How awkward it felt, this wall that had been built between them. "I love the new song."

"Thank you." His gaze slowly slid over her in a way that made her nipples harden and heat sweep low into her groin. "How are you, Nic?"

Though she had promised herself she would spare no tears, she felt them burning the backs of her eyes. The reunion she had envisioned had not happened and she was devastated. He had gone on with his life. He did not have a place for her in it. "I am well. Charlotte has been very good to me."

"I'm glad." He took a sip of champagne, watching her over the rim the entire time. "And your father? It seems he has let all the skeletons out of his closet."

Nicolette let her gaze slip to his cravat and the diamond stud there. No doubt a bounty from the money her father had given him. "Yes, he's happy to have a child."

He frowned. "I thought you would stay with him."

She shook her head. "No, that would be too awkward."

"And Darian?"

She flinched. "Salvatore, it's not what it seems. I had no idea that they would announce our engagement. I have not even seen him since Kedgwick Manor."

His jaw clenched and his gaze searched hers. "He wasted no time getting rid of Elizabeth, did he?"

"I was as shocked as you were."

"Truly?" There was something in his eyes that told her he did not believe her. Did he think she had slept with Darian?

She bristled beneath that stare. "*Yes*, I was."

The pianist who played with him, Nicolette's replacement, came up then, interrupting them. There was so much she wanted to say to him, to tell him that she and Darian had never been intimate. "Salvatore, you must meet Sir Percy, the man I told you about earlier this week. The one who would like us to play at his daughter's wedding," the girl gushed, embracing him like Nicolette wanted to do.

"Of course. Will you excuse me for a moment?" he asked, before the woman drug him off.

Nicolette watched him leave with a wave of disappointment and sadness. The easy playfulness they had always had, had now disappeared. The room took on a stifling quality, to the point Nicolette needed to get away, out of the room.

She raced down the hallway, into the lobby and out the front entrance, forgetting her cloak.

The cool air rushed up to greet her, and she welcomed it. Her cheeks were hot, as were the tears that would not stop.

"My lady, may I call you a carriage?" a footman asked, and she shook her head, wiping away at the tears. She raced across the street, not caring she was alone or that it was night.

A hand clasped onto her shoulder and she let out a shriek.

"Nic, where are you going?"

Salvatore embraced her from behind, his body hard against her back. His strong arms enfolded her. She could feel his heart pounding frantically against her.

"Where are you going?" he asked again, his voice soft, his breath hot against her ear.

"I don't know."

He turned her in his arms, and she could see the concern in his golden eyes. This was the Salvatore she knew and loved. The man she had fallen in love with, without even realizing it. Flashing a tender smile, he cupped her jaw with his hands. "Forgive me. *Forgive me.* I am behaving like a jealous lover, and yet I have no right."

Her heart leapt at the declaration.

"God, how I have missed you."

She wept with relief. "And I you."

She touched the hand that still palmed her jaw and brought it to her lips. The smile that had been in place moments before had now disappeared.

Without a word, he lifted her in his arms and strode toward a carriage. The footman scrambled down and opened the door for them. Salvatore sat, and still held her on his lap. "To Drury Lane."

"Drury Lane? You don't mean…"

He smiled. "Yes, we're going home, Nic."

Chapter Eighteen

✌

Many of the faces had changed at Madame la Monte's. The brothel's interior however had not. Still the red tacky velvet curtains, the overstuffed furniture strategically placed in dark corners, away from prying eyes.

Thankfully Salvatore's and Nicolette's arrival had gone unnoticed, except by Madame la Monte herself, who gave a loud shriek when they'd entered through the back door. She had raced over and embraced Nicolette, her perfume nearly choking her as much as the hug. The boisterous woman had changed very little, save for more lines around her mouth and eyes.

Salvatore led Nicolette to the large corner room he rented. One would never guess it to be in a brothel, for the room held an elegance that Nic had seen in some of the grandest hotels of Europe. Posh creams, golds, warm-colored walls.

Nicolette sat on the bed, watching as Salvatore removed his jacket and hung it over a chair. Her heart constricted. She could hardly believe she was with him. "Why did you return here?"

He looked about the room, a hint of a smile on his lips. "I wanted to be closer to you."

Touched, she returned his smile and watched as he walked toward her, his gaze roving over her, telling her with that look alone that she had not been the only one who had suffered their parting. In the carriage ride he had held her tight, not kissing her, saying nothing as his thumb brushed over her wrist again and again. And she had closed her eyes, taking in the comfort of being back in his arms.

Stopping before her, he reached out for her hand. She took it, and he helped her to her feet.

She went up on her toes and kissed him, tentatively at first. With a groan, he deepened the kiss, a hand closing over her breast, playing with her nipple through the material. Her stomach tightened as heat radiated from where he touched her, down to the apex of her thighs. She burned for him.

Reaching between them, she ripped his shirt from his pants. He smiled against her lips, before pulling away to rid himself of his clothing.

How beautiful he was in all his masculine glory, the muscles of his stomach tightening, his long, thick sex jutting out proudly.

She offered him her back, and he made quick work of the buttons, kissing her shoulder as he drew the gown from her. It fell in a puddle at her feet. "I can scarcely believe my eyes," he said, already tugging at the strings of her corset.

"Charlotte insists that I wear one."

"You have become a young lady in my absence."

She glanced at him over her shoulder. "Only when absolutely necessary."

"That's my girl." Kissing her bare shoulder, he flung the corset aside, then did the same with her chemise. Enfolding her in his arms, she smiled, insanely happy.

"I thought never to return here."

"I know. I never wanted to come back, yet now I suddenly wish we could stay here forever."

She looked up at him. "You knew I wouldn't look here. That's why you came?"

"Forgive me?"

She did not bring up the money Simon had paid him. She could not bear to.

Going up on the tips of her toes, she kissed him. "The time for talking is through."

With a gentle tug, she pulled him on top of her as they toppled onto the mattress. His long hair fell against her face and she inhaled the fresh scent, her fingers weaving through the silky strands.

He kissed her, once, twice, before his lips traveled over her chin, down her throat, over her quivering breasts. His tongue stroked a diamond-hard nipple, teasing it into a pointed peak before moving to the other.

Her hands explored his strong back, feeling the muscle beneath her fingertips. She gasped as his lips kissed a path from her breasts to her stomach, his tongue laving her navel. Nicolette's stomach tightened, her hands clenched his head.

He moved down, between her thighs. He brought his hands beneath her buttocks, lifting her to his mouth.

"Salvatore…"

He grinned wickedly before his tongue stroked her.

Nicolette's breath left her in a rush. She had never in her life experienced such wicked pleasure. It seemed he knew where to touch her, how to touch her, and in a way that made her entire body sing.

Unconsciously, she opened her legs wider. How wicked it was to watch him pleasure her, taking her excitement to a higher place. His long lashes fanned against high cheekbones, his silky hair caressing her thighs, his full lips, his long tongue making her writhe blissfully.

Her body tightened, her blood roared, and she could feel the start of her climax, building as she reached for the stars, ever higher, exploding into a million pieces, drifting back down to Earth and to reality.

Salvatore bowed over her, looking down at her, the sweetest smile on his lips. He kissed her, and for a moment she was horrified that she dare taste herself. Yet there was nothing horrible about it. In fact, it made her feel closer to him, to be able to share something so intimate…so wonderful.

His hard shaft pressed against her sensitive folds, seeking entrance. With a single thrust he filled her completely. He moved slowly, his strokes controlled, and then in the blink of an eye he rolled, to where she was now astride him in the dominant position.

He grinned wolfishly as his hands moved to her breasts, palming them, and he sat up a little, taking one into his mouth. Nicolette moved her hips experimentally, enjoying the control she had, the myriad sensations with him cradled inside her, and his lips on her breasts.

Long fingers braced about her hips and he lifted her, showing her the pace, teaching her what to do.

Once she overcame the initial shock of being in control, she found she loved riding him, building a pace that made her breath quicken and her body pulse.

"You feel so good," he said between gritted teeth.

"So do you," she said, pushing him back against the pillows, entwining her fingers with his.

She felt him swell within her, thicker, longer, stretching her. Letting her head fall back on her shoulders she allowed herself to let go. To do nothing but feel, to savor the moment and to celebrate it.

His hands moved to her hips, urging her on. His soft moans told her he was near, and she was following quickly behind.

Then he came. His fingers tightened about her hips and he lifted his hips. How beautiful he was in the throes of passion. Feeling his hot seed fill her, Nicolette climaxed, and fell on top of him, sated and complete.

* * * * *

Salvatore woke to an empty bed.

In a glance he saw Nicolette had left. His gaze skipped over the room, looking for a note, but he found nothing.

He dressed quickly, and raced downstairs. There was no one about this morning, all the girls sleeping the day away until night. The only sound came by way of Solomon, the old Negro who had worked at Madame La Monte's for an eternity, it seemed. The old man hummed as he dusted the banister. Seeing him, Solomon nodded. "Good morning, sir!"

"Have you seen Nicolette?"

The old man's brows furrowed. "I can't say that I have."

Salvatore patted the man on the back and headed toward the attic stairway. The narrow passage was barely three feet wide, and very steep. Salvatore's fingers brushed the walls with open familiarity as he ascended. How many times had he and Nicolette walked this path? Would she be there now?

Salvatore pushed open the door and looked about the cramped room, disappointed that Nicolette wasn't there. The room was dark, save for a bit of light shining through the small window. It had always seemed small before, but now it was suffocating. And to think the two of them had lived here for years, every day yearning for something better. Yearning for escape.

There was a cot in one corner, a piece of broken glass hanging on the wall, serving as a mirror, and a rickety old table where an old volume sat. His fingers skimmed over the gold lettering. *Gulliver's Travels*. He smiled, remembering reading the story to Nicolette night after night. He had not been able to bring himself to come here before. He could not have handled the memories, the wanting to see her, and knowing she could no longer be a part of her life.

What would become of them now?

If Simon had his way, he would make certain he never saw Nicolette again. And what of Darian? Salvatore had already been cut from many guest lists. It was a matter of time before all doors closed to him and Nicolette. Perhaps they could return to their villa in Greece. Stay there forever.

Salvatore had had no intention of making love to Nicolette last night. Her presence at the ball had been a surprise, yet secretly he had hoped for her to be there. Though he had promised himself he would not return to London, the offer to play at the annual ball had been too generous.

With memories of their childhood dancing in his mind, Salvatore walked to the wall and lifted the small mirror. He smiled. The initials N.L. and S.T. were still there. He ran his fingers over the rugged letters, remembering the night they had done so.

He gave the room one more glance before turning around and heading back down the way he'd come. Where had Nicolette gone to, and why had she not said goodbye?

* * * * *

As luck would have it Darian had arrived at Charlotte's townhouse a mere ten minutes before Nicolette.

Wearing her gown from the evening before, Nicolette entered the parlor. Charlotte, who had been staring out the window, turned at her entrance, as did Darian who crossed the room in long strides. "There you are!" He stopped in midstride. "You are wearing the same gown you had on last night."

Accusation laced every single word.

Darian's gaze raked her from head to toe. "Where the hell have you been?"

"I stayed over with a friend."

The nerve in his jaw twitched. "And which friend would that be, or need I ask?"

Nicolette looked from him to Charlotte, then back again. "I daresay that is none of your business."

"It is very much my business." His dark eyes were not at all warm. "You are my fiancée, Nicolette, or have you forgotten that?"

"I told you last night that I have no intention of marrying you," Nicolette said, stepping past him to take a seat beside Charlotte, "and I have not changed my mind."

"You think you will receive a better offer?" Disbelief laced each word.

"Darian, I understand your anger toward me, and there is nothing I can say that will excuse what I had planned to do to you and Elizabeth at the engagement party, but nothing came of it. I don't understand your hatred toward your brother. He did nothing to you."

Darian snorted. "You call his intention to destroy me nothing!"

"He did *not* destroy you. In fact, why would you even choose to marry me, given the fact *I* was as guilty in the plan as Salvatore?"

He opened his mouth, then snapped it shut again.

"Exactly!"

"Your father has given me his blessing, and we have already announced it to the *Ton*. The banns were posted yesterday and will be in every publication come Saturday morning."

"I'm sorry you and Simon went to such lengths to undermine me, but it still does not change my mind. I will not, now or anytime in the future, marry you."

"You have little choice in the matter, Nicolette. I have told your father that you could already possibly be carrying my child."

"But that is a lie."

His gaze shifted from hers to her breasts. "You have gained weight, Nicolette, and everyone at the house party knows what you had intended — or should I say — Salvatore had intended. You were innocent in his plot to ruin me."

Nicolette could not believe the man had the audacity to tell her that she would marry him. "I don't care what you say, the answer is, and will always be no."

"You will be ruined."

"Come, Darian, don't embarrass yourself further," Charlotte said, reaching for her teacup. "Your threats are quite tiresome and I thought more of you."

"What do you know?" he quipped.

Charlotte lifted her brows. "Apparently more than you do. For the love of God, do you think every woman you meet will fall at your feet?"

"You always opened your legs for me, my dear," he said with a sneer.

Charlotte smirked. "Yes, and you never turned me down either. Even last night you had me in your carriage and you finished within seconds, so do not act the martyr in front of Nicolette. She's being honest with you. The least you can do is give her the same courtesy."

Darian stammered, his cheeks turning red. "You all but threw yourself at me."

Charlotte rolled her eyes. "Mutual desire is always an asset in any friendship."

"Spoken like a true whore."

Nicolette very nearly tossed her tea in his face.

"You are such a hypocrite, Darian. No doubt you've fucked every actress from here to Italy...and you call me a whore?" Charlotte shook her head. "Aside from Charles and two other men, you are the only other person I've ever been intimate with." She lifted her chin. "I can count my lovers on one hand. Can you say the same?"

Darian frowned. "You lie."

"Get me a Bible. I will swear upon it," Charlotte said with conviction, and Nicolette did not doubt her friend for one moment.

Nicolette glanced from one to the other. They were both furious, but at least their attention and aggression had been turned on each other.

Salvatore walked in, and all three of them stopped and turned to the door.

Nicolette's heart skittered. Dressed in a navy suit, his long hair tied back in a queue, he was so handsome it almost hurt to look at him.

"I'm sorry to just walk into your home, Charlotte. I heard arguing, so I nearly ran your footman down in my haste."

"You are always welcome," Charlotte said, nodding toward the older footman who just now entered, looking none too pleased with Salvatore. "Please bring us another cup of tea, Alfred."

"Well, if it isn't the bastard," Darian said, shaking his head. "You have the audacity to show your face here."

"What in the hell is that supposed to mean?" Charlotte replied. "Salvatore is *always* welcome in my home. That is more than I can say about you, Lord Kedgwick."

"Lord Kedgwick, is it?"

"I came to visit Nicolette," Salvatore said. He walked straight to her, took her hand in his and brought it to his lips. "Good morning, my dear."

Nicolette could feel a blush race up her cheeks. The wicked things they had done last night coming back to her in detail. How delicious making love to him had been. As his golden eyes stared into hers, she was reminded of how heavy-lidded they had been when he had looked at her as she rode him. "Good morning."

"Simon does not want you around his daughter," Darian said, his eyes narrowed.

Salvatore glanced at Darian. "Simon does not have a say in how I lead my life."

Darian smirked. "Is that so?"

"Indeed, it is."

"He paid you to disappear."

Nicolette swallowed hard. Darian had managed to bring up the one thing she had been too afraid to ask last night.

Salvatore kissed her hand before walking toward his brother. They were both of the same height, and Salvatore stopped mere inches from him. "Do you mean this note?" he asked, pulling it from his wallet.

Darian ripped the note from Salvatore's hand. He looked at it, then to Salvatore. "You didn't cash it?"

Salvatore shook his head. "Of course not. I told him I would not be bought, and I won't be."

"Yet you carry it in your pocket. Were you waiting for the right time?" Darian asked smugly.

Salvatore smiled. "No, I wanted it as a reminder to how devious a bastard both you and Lord Wellesley are."

"Trust me when I say you will wish you had, because no one of *the ton* will invite you into their homes once they discover the truth."

"What? That my father was a womanizing bastard who made promises to my mother that he would never keep. He would throw her aside, leave her pregnant and broke, to make her own way on the streets of London. I was five years old when I saw him for the first time. A broken man who did not resemble the picture my mother always carried with her. He said he came to see for himself the bastard that he had sired. He looked at me, proclaimed me to be 'too exotic looking' to be his son, then, slapping my mother and calling her a whore, he left. My mother never again was the same."

A nerve twitched in Darian's cheek. "I know nothing of my father's bastards."

"You should. I'm certain the continent is littered with them."

"But *I* am the heir."

Salvatore shook his head. "And to think I once envied you for being his legitimate son. Now all I feel for you is pity."

"You lie if you say you wish you did not have a father."

"I *do* have a father, and his name is Count de Vassey and he lives in France."

Darian frowned. "I know this de Vassey you speak of."

Salvatore smiled. "Yes, I know you do. He commented on meeting you once in Paris. He said you were the boy with the sad eyes."

Darian bristled under Salvatore's gaze. "Foolish man!"

"You hated our father as well. I can not blame you for that. He was not a very good man."

Darian grabbed hold of Salvatore by the throat.

"Let go of him!" Charlotte yelled, ringing for her footman, but by the time he arrived, Salvatore had escaped his brother's clutches and held a dagger at his throat.

Salvatore relented, sheathing his dagger once more. "I am not proud of what I intended to do to you, and believe it or not, there was a day I yearned to have a brother such as yourself. In fact, I would still like to have a brother, but I fear that bridge has been burned."

"I suggest you leave,"

"I shall, now that I have the woman I came for."

"Nicolette is leaving with *me*," Darian said.

Nicolette shook her head. "Darian, as I've told you before, you have no say over what I do. Plus, I love Salvatore, and he's the man I will be with."

Darian smiled sardonically. "You will be sorry. What will *you* do for money? You'll be ruined by week's end."

Nicolette looked at Salvatore and they shared a smile. "We have always managed to survive. We will do so now."

"For now you have a career. But how long will that last when the *Ton* discovers who you really are, and what you were going to do. We are a tight-knit group, watching each other's backs. They are the ones who pay your way, and once they learn the truth, you will not be able to play in even the shoddiest theaters of Covent Garden."

Nicolette's stomach tightened.

"You are such an ass," Charlotte replied, planting her hands on her hips. "I am so ashamed of you right now."

"Nicolette, I will give you the life you want, the life you deserve. He can give you nothing."

Nearly choking from her anger, Nicolette shook her head. "I have the life I want. I always have. Yes, we did something stupid because we hated what our fathers had done to us. If I could take back the stupid guise, I would. But we have apologized already, and no harm was done."

Darian snorted. "Perhaps in your eyes."

"Oh for God's sake, Darian," Charlotte blurted.

"You have no idea who you are dealing with," Darian said, running a hand through his hair. "You have no idea of the power I wield."

"I have heard enough," Charlotte said, heading for the door and throwing it open right as Alfred arrived, his eyes huge in his weathered face, a pistol in his trembling hand. Charlotte took it from the old man's hand and aimed it at Darian. "Darian, get the hell out, before I throw you out...or worse."

Clearly startled by the turn of events, Darian walked toward Nicolette and Salvatore.

"You will be sorry you denied me, Nicolette," Darian said, and with that threat, he left them.

Salvatore hugged her to him. "I think it is safe to say we have worn out our welcome in London."

Charlotte handed the gun to Alfred and turned to them. "I am afraid what Simon is going to do now, Nicolette. Darian is one thing, but Simon is another threat altogether. He will not take this slight well, particularly since he took a chance in introducing you to society as his daughter. For you to flee London with a musician, and I mean you no disrespect, Salvatore."

Salvatore nodded. "None taken."

"Particularly the day after your engagement to one of the most eligible men in England…"

"I am the same person I always was—"

Reaching out to Nicolette, Charlotte grabbed hold of her hand. "And I am not saying this to hurt you, or to make you feel remorseful. Lord knows Darian has done a fine job of that already. Perhaps you should leave while you can. Leave London before Simon catches word. Lord knows, that should be any minute."

Chapter Nineteen

❧

Nicolette woke up in their room at Madame la Monte's. Salvatore stood near the open window, leaning out, his lean body bare to the waist. As he moved, the muscle and sinew played beneath his olive skin.

She smiled, remembering how he had held her throughout the night. They had not made love, both too content just to know that their world was once again right, and that they had each other.

Neither one of them brought up Darian's threat, but they both realized he had the power to destroy them. Nicolette had little doubt every drawing room in London would be teeming with the news by week's end.

Salvatore shut the window, then sat down near the fire. He picked up his pen, dipped it in the ink and began to write. She had always loved the process he went through when writing. He appeared to be in another world, a place so intense, that often times when he looked at her, he seemed to see right through her.

Slowly she got up from the bed, holding her breath as not to make a noise.

She tiptoed toward him, and was just three steps away, when he reached out and grabbed her, pulling her onto his lap.

"How did you know I was awake?"

He grinned wickedly. "I could feel you watching me when I peered out the window."

She glanced around behind him.

"What?" he asked, brows furrowed into a frown.

"I was checking to see if you had eyes in the back of your head."

He shook his head and kissed her. "Silly girl. Would you like some tea?"

She shook her head. "No, but I do have a craving."

"And what would that be?" he asked, wrapping a curl about his finger.

Licking her bottom lip, she tried to look as innocent as possible. When she wiggled her bottom, he grinned wolfishly.

"Ah, I think I understand."

Before he could blink she straddled him in the chair. The smile that had been there moments before disappeared as she kissed his mouth, then his nose, one eyelid, then the other. His eyes remained closed as she rained kisses along his jaw, then his ear. She licked the lobe, then the curve, before stroking the inside ridge.

His hands moved to her hips, pulling her up against him, against the hard length of his cock.

He bent down and laved a nipple through the silk fabric of her chemise. Delicious bursts of pleasure rippled through her. Wrapping her arms about his broad shoulders, she rotated her hips.

He wrenched the chemise from her and threw it aside. The only thing between them was his pants. With one hand he unbuttoned them, not bothering to break contact with her.

Shifting her hips again, she smiled, noting the fine sheen of sweat on his brow.

He lifted her then, and set her on his thick rod. The breath caught in her throat as she took in inch after delicious inch, until he was buried deep inside her.

Never had he looked so beautiful to her as he did then, gazing at her with love in his eyes. He palmed a breast and played with a sensitive nipple. "Your breasts are bigger than they used to be."

"I am a woman now, Salvatore," she teased, kissing him again.

"I know that well, my dear," he whispered against her mouth, his lips traveling down her neck, to the tops of her breasts.

Her body quickened, white-hot fire racing through her veins, and she moved against him, her body pulsing with the force of her orgasm.

Salvatore felt her sheath tighten around him like a clenched fist, surprised how quickly she'd climaxed. Her sweet cries were like music to his ears. He picked her up, still joined and laid her on the bed. He stood at the edge of the bed, looking down at her. Her cheeks were flushed, her mouth open, her full breasts rising and falling as she caught her breath.

He pulled out, teasing her with the head of his cock. She bit into her bottom lip. Smiling, he inched into her, and her thighs fell open wider to receive him.

With heart hammering loud in his chest, he let his hands wander up over the sensitive skin between thigh and groin, then higher to her belly, which swelled slightly.

His gaze shifted to her large, full breasts and a thought occurred to him.

"Nicolette, are you with child?"

His heart skipped a beat, for he knew by the look on her face he had guessed right. She watched him tentatively, waiting for his reaction.

His child! Nicolette would have his child!

The news filled him with an immense joy, and he leaned over her, kissing her with all the love he felt for her.

* * * * *

Salvatore was so quiet.

He had been that way since yesterday when she had told him about their baby. It had been obvious by his smile and sudden gentleness as they'd made love, that he had been pleased by the news…yet there had been something in his eyes that told her he was concerned.

No doubt his thoughts were on Darian, and what he could do to their career. When it was the two of them they had not worried, figuring they could always find work somewhere in Europe. But that life was not conducive to raising a child and they both knew it.

Even a few months from now, traveling would be difficult, and she had little doubt Salvatore would be content to stay in one place. He always grew restless. Having a child would not change that. Would he leave, travel, entertain, while she stayed home with the child?

She flinched at the thought of such a separation.

Salvatore set his violin aside.

"You have been so quiet."

He turned, almost as though he were surprised she was there. How distracted he had been.

A knock sounded at the door, and he jumped up to get it. Nicolette could hear the girl, one of Madame la Monte's new whores, who did not like Nicolette at all. Nicolette did not have to guess at the reason, and though she wanted to ask Salvatore if he had slept with the pretty redhead during their separation, she could not bear to hear the answer.

Shifting the slightest bit, so she could see the woman, Nicolette bit back a curse. The girl, wearing nothing save a chemise, wound a red curl about her finger as she handed Salvatore a letter. Her large nipples were clearly visible through the fabric, and Nicolette could see from where she sat that the girl had no drawers on beneath.

"Thank you, Nalise," Salvatore said, shutting the door.

"What is it?" Nicolette asked, trying to keep the jealousy out of her tone, but failing.

The side of Salvatore's mouth lifted, as though knowing she bristled. "It is from Charlotte."

Salvatore handed it to her, and sat down beside her on the bed.

Nicolette scanned the letter. Her heart dropped. Darian was out for blood. He was calling Salvatore out at dawn on the morrow.

"We have to leave London," she said, crumpling the letter in her hand.

Salvatore lifted her chin with gentle fingers. "Nicolette, I will not run from my brother. If he wants to meet me on the field at dawn, I am more than ready to appease him."

"No!"

"You do not think I can best him?" Though the words were said in jest, Nicolette heard the hurt in his voice. She had seen for herself that Darian was skilled with bow and arrow, and though Salvatore had bested him in that sport, she did not know if he was even more skilled with a gun.

"I will not lose you."

"I am not going anywhere, Nicolette." His hand rested on her abdomen. "We cannot keep running forever. We are being given a chance with our son or daughter. If we can not play in London, then I will teach here—or anywhere else in the world."

"But what if—"

Salvatore put his finger to her lips. "No more 'what if's. We will take each day as it comes without always looking over our shoulders."

Chapter Twenty

ౚ

The morning was cold and dreary, the wet grass making the ground slippery. Not the best conditions for a duel.

Salvatore had woken early, making sure to be so quiet that Nicolette would not wake and follow him here.

She had begged him to not come, to make a public apology to Darian, so that they could move on with their lives.

He had held her and assured her that he would talk with his brother. Yet now, as the sun rose on the horizon, he had little to say. He had bared his soul, and his brother knew why he had tried to end his marriage to Elizabeth. He had wanted revenge on their father, period. Salvatore knew that this duel had nothing to do with their father, and everything to do with Nicolette.

Darian Tremayne never knew what it was like to not get his way, and Nicolette served as a bitter reminder that money could not buy happiness.

"The Earl of Kedgwick is here," Solomon said, the old Negro looking more nervous than Salvatore felt. Secretly he had yearned for this day when he could meet his brother on equal footing. He knew Darian dueled often, his rakish behavior causing many husbands of *the ton* to reclaim their wives' honor.

Salvatore's heart thumped loudly. The black carriage with the golden kedgwick crest rolled along the gravel drive and came to a stop. Salvatore took off his coat just as Darian stepped out of the carriage.

He looked like he had not slept at all. In fact, it appeared he was still dressed as he had been yesterday. Darian stumbled, nearly fell to the ground, but for his friend, Viscount Athenry, who steadied him, looking a bit out of sorts himself.

They were drunk.

"There you are," Darian said, a sardonic smile on his face. "I thought for certain you would not show."

How arrogant he was, this brother of his. Nay, a brother he would never be.

Darian managed to get out of his coat, though with help from his second, Lord Athenry. He glanced at Salvatore, then looked to Solomon. The side of his mouth lifted in a sneer. "*This* is your second?"

Solomon went still at Salvatore's side. "I need no second. This is between you and me, and no substitute will be accepted."

The viscount released a relieved breath, obviously grateful to have been let off so easily.

Another gentleman, this one much older than Darian, motioned for them to follow him to the field. He opened a case and nodded to Salvatore. "His lordship has been good enough to give you first choice of weapons."

Salvatore took the closest sleek-handled gun.

Darian took the other, his hand trembling the slightest bit. Salvatore wondered if it was from drink or nerves.

"Get into position—back to back. You will walk ten paces, and at my signal, you will turn and fire."

Salvatore's heart pounded so loudly it was a roar in his ears. Thoughts of Nicolette raced through his mind, and the image of their baby, wondering if he or she would favor their beautiful mother in both looks and spirit. He smiled inwardly, knowing that if he died this day, he would do so a lucky man.

He could only pray that he would make it from this field alive, and once he did, he would put the past behind him once and for all. If he did not live, he could only hope that Simon Laurent would take care of Nicolette and their baby.

"One, two, three…"

Salvatore took each step, the pistol cold and heavy in his hand.

"Eight, nine, ten."

The signal had not yet been given when Salvatore heard the blast of a pistol and felt a searing pain through his right shoulder.

* * * * *

Inside the elaborate carriage belonging to her father, Nicolette tried to remain calm as best she could. The sun had just set, and she feared the worst.

She was furious that Salvatore had left her at the brothel without saying a word, and more importantly, for doing what just last night he had promised he would not do.

God she prayed she was not too late.

She had roused her father from his sleep, his valet looking none-too-happy to be receiving callers so early. Simon, in his haste, threw on his overcoat, called for his carriage to be brought around, and joined Nicolette in the carriage.

"My dear, I just hope we are not too late."

She frowned, not liking her fears voiced aloud.

"I am pregnant, Simon."

He blinked a few times. "Pardon?"

Swallowing hard against the tightness in her throat, Nicolette repeated, "I am pregnant."

He studied her, his eyes narrowing. "It is Darian's child?"

"Of course it's not Darian's. I have never been with him in that way."

"But he told me that you could be pregnant with his child."

No wonder he had been so quick to announce her engagement before *the ton*. Darian had done so in order to get

225

out of his engagement to Elizabeth, and to get her in his bed. "I swear to you, I have only been with one man, and that man is –"

"Salvatore," he finished for her, squeezing the bridge of his nose between finger and thumb. "No wonder you were so adamant about not marrying Darian. I could not understand it. Damn, Kedgwick. That young man has always manipulated people, much like his father had."

"I thought you were friends?"

"I knew the previous earl quite well. In truth, we ran in the same circles and even traveled abroad, but he changed after university. He seemed more corrupt, and I thought the way he treated his wife was deplorable."

Nicolette flinched. Talk about the pot calling the kettle black.

"I know I have little room to talk, but know this much, Nicolette. I did love your mother, very much so. I wanted to believe that you were my child, yet she told me you were not…and I believed her. I suppose I cannot blame her. I had married by then, and she feared losing you to me, which she could have done, particularly when Henrietta and I remained childless."

Out of the corner of her eye, Nicolette saw a carriage. "Oh my goodness, is that Salvatore?" Nicolette said, squinting out at the passing landscape. "Yes, there they are!"

"Stop!" Simon yelled, and the carriage stopped. Simon flung open the carriage door, and Nicolette rushed out…and then a shot fired.

And Salvatore stumbled, then fell to his knees.

"No!" she screamed, her heart hammering as she ran.

Simon reached for her. "Nicolette, he is alive. He stirs. In fact, he is coming to his feet."

Sure enough, Salvatore stood. He shook his head as though to clear it.

Nicolette held her breath, watching as Salvatore turned to face his brother, who paled, his dark eyes wide with fear.

Darian's hand trembled, barely holding onto the smoking pistol, which he had shot before the signal had been given.

Simon wrapped his arm about her waist. "It is Salvatore's turn, and Darian must not move."

Salvatore reached up to his wounded shoulder, wiped the blood there, and shook his head. He took a deep breath and lifted the pistol.

Darian trembled like a leaf. No doubt he had not been in this position before. Now he faced his greatest foe yet — his bastard brother, a man who had done nothing to him, save give him what he had wanted most, and that was a way out of a marriage he would never have been able to tolerate.

"I can not bear it," Nicolette whispered.

"Salvatore shall be fine, my dear."

Though she disliked the spoiled and mean-spirited Darian, she didn't wish him dead. However, she knew what would happen if Salvatore missed.

Viscount Athenry stood, mouth open in horror. It seemed he too had not foreseen this turn of events.

Salvatore cocked the gun, pulled the trigger, shifting his aim at the last second, and firing into the air.

Darian fell to his knees, his breath coming in gasps. The viscount made a shrill sound before running a hand over his face. Salvatore stood where he was.

Simon clapped his hands, and Salvatore and Darian looked to him. "Well done, Salvatore."

"It is Kedgwick's turn to shoot," the viscount said, his voice tinged with excitement.

"This duel is finished." Your friend is lucky that he did not lose his life this day. Not only did he pull the trigger before the signal was given, his brother spared him his life." Simon nodded for the surgeon to help Salvatore.

"His brother?" the viscount said, his gaze raking over Salvatore. "You can not mean that he," he motioned to Salvatore, "is Kedgwick's brother?"

"Indeed, that is exactly what I mean. Salvatore is the son of Franklin Tremayne, and younger brother to Darian."

"So…that is why he wanted to stop the wedding."

Salvatore lay propped against a tree, and Nicolette kneeled down beside him while the surgeon checked the wound. "It is quite deep, but I think I can feel the bullet," he said, removing his gloves and probing the wound with his fingers.

Nicolette kissed Salvatore's cheek. "Squeeze my hand as tight as you must. Do not bear this alone."

He smiled a little, wincing when the doctor probed yet again. "I can honestly say that I will never duel again."

"Is that a promise?"

He kissed her softly, then squeezed her hand so tight, she flinched. "Sorry, my love."

How grateful she was to have him. And how grateful she was to her father. If they had not arrived, lord only knows what would have happened.

Darian came to his feet slowly. He handed the pistol to Solomon, ran a hand through his hair and approached Salvatore. Nicolette thought he looked not only exhausted, but embarrassed, as well he should be. His cowardice had been a shock and a surprise. She had not thought it possible for a man to sink so low as to jump the signal and shoot a man when his back was still turned.

He should be ashamed.

"Will he be all right?" Darian asked the surgeon, who lifted a brow and nodded.

Darian nodded, and without another word, left the field.

* * * * *

Charlotte and Nicolette worked on a baby blanket, both content to sit before the fire.

"It is snowing."

Nicolette glanced over at Salvatore, who had stopped practicing, set his violin and bow aside, and opened the window. He had a hand over his wound, and though he winced as he looked out, he smiled. "Look, the flakes are enormous. Come, get your wrap and let's go out."

She grinned. Salvatore had always loved the snow. Even as a child he would race to get hat and gloves, going out to play for hours, and returning red-nosed but gleefully happy.

"You think me foolish?" he asked, walking over to her and kissing her.

"Never," she replied, savoring the feel of his arms embracing her.

Charlotte's valet, Alfred, cleared his throat loudly. "There is a visitor, my lady."

The words had no more left his mouth when Darian walked in, brushing snowflakes off his coat.

Charlotte jumped to her feet, letting the blanket fall to the ground. "Darian! You are not welcome here! Go, before I have you thrown out."

"I have need to speak with Salvatore."

"There is nothing to say," Charlotte said, blocking his way.

Darian looked at Salvatore. "Oh, but I am afraid there is. Please, may I have a word with you privately."

"Whatever you have to say can be said amongst Nicolette and Charlotte."

Two bright spots bloomed on Darian's cheeks. "I have come to apologize for my behavior toward you. I have been unjust."

"That is an understatement," Charlotte murmured, covering it with a cough when Darian glanced her way.

"I am not proud of shooting you before the signal. I have to blame it on the night of drinking. If I had my wits about me, I would not have done so. I would have played by the rules, as honorable men do."

Salvatore nodded.

"I know little of who you are, Salvatore, but I do know that my father had talked about you."

Salvatore squeezed Nicolette's hand.

"He told my mother and me of a woman he loved dearly. He said that she was a gypsy woman whom he had met while on holiday in Greece with friends. He was engaged to my mother at the time, a match of the realm of course, but he loved your mother." Darian ran a hand through his hair, and Nicolette could see he trembled. "My mother hated him for telling her that there was someone else. She knew he had taken mistresses, but never had he mentioned love…until he spoke of your mother."

"May I?" he asked, pointing to a chair, and Charlotte nodded. They all sat down and waited as Darian shrugged out of his coat. "He told me that I had a brother, a young man with gold eyes and a smile that could charm anyone. I forgot about that until recently. I am amazed it took me so long to figure out that you were my brother."

Alfred entered with a tea trolley, and Darian clamped his lips together, waiting patiently as the old man served tea. When he shut the door behind him, Darian took a drink of tea, then set it down. "I am sorry for the sins of my father." He shook his head. "*Our* father."

Nicolette knew what it took for Darian to utter those words. He cleared his throat and stood. "I am sorry for what I have done to you. We spoke before of not having siblings, particularly a brother. Yet we do, and I think it would a horrible waste if we kept things as they are. I do not want to be your enemy, and I have to believe that you do not want me as your enemy."

Salvatore nodded. "Indeed, I do not."

"Then please accept my forgiveness and let us begin anew." He walked over to Salvatore and extended his hand.

Salvatore took his brother's hand and shook it. Darian pulled him into his arms and for the first time the brothers hugged, though it looked as awkward as it no doubt felt.

Nicolette grinned at Charlotte, who had tears shining in her eyes.

Putting Salvatore at arm's length, Darian glanced over at Nicolette. "I have had ample time to think on some of the things you said. I have not been very wise when it comes to the women in my life." He turned to Charlotte. "The woman I have needed has been standing before me the entire time, and I have been a fool."

Charlotte's mouth dropped open. "Darian, you can not mean—especially after treating me as horrible as you have."

"My dearest, Charlotte, I will spend the rest of our lives making up for it," he said, pulling her into his arms and kissing her.

Chapter Twenty-One

✍

Nicolette soaked in the tub and looked at her husband who lounged before the fire. He wore just his pants, having done away with his jacket, waistcoast and shirt long ago. The wedding had been a long affair, the reception even longer, and they had danced until their feet ached, celebrating with their family.

Saying goodbye had been more difficult than Nicolette had imagined. She had always traveled, was always used to goodbyes yet now it seemed...different. And she knew why. They had been running for so long, they had not understood that they had been running from themselves.

Now, they had found out who they were, and there was nothing or no one to run from. Rather, they now had family to run to.

And as strange as it was, it felt good.

As though sensing her perusal, Salvatore glanced over at her, a lazy smile on his lips. "Are you happy?"

She grinned. "I'm blissfully happy."

He came to his feet, and she drank in the sight of him. He unbuttoned his pants as he came toward her, with an animal-like quality that sent her heart racing.

He pushed the pants down over his narrow hips, over muscled thighs and calves, and then kicked them aside. Making quick work of his drawers, he stood before her in all his naked glory, a wicked gleam in his eye.

"You are not thinking of joining me, are you?" she asked, though she very much hoped that was the case.

232

He lifted a dark brow. "Do you not think there is enough room for us both?"

Frowning, she shook her head. "I fear the tub is much too small, especially since I am growing larger by the day."

"I love all your curves, and your glorious breasts," he said, weighing them in his hands as he kissed the top of each globe. "In fact, I may keep you pregnant always."

He lifted her effortlessly, water sluicing down her body and onto the floor.

"Salvatore, the rug."

"Will dry," he said, kissing her hard as he laid her down upon the rug before the fire, drying her with a fluffy towel.

He lay beside her, going up on his elbow, looking down at her. "I am the luckiest man in the world," he said, leaning over her, kissing her belly and laying his cheek there.

Nicolette looked down at her beloved, the smile on his face, the joy in his eyes.

The future was theirs for the taking.

"If it is a boy, I would like to call him Simon."

Nicolette searched his face. "Do you mean it?"

He nodded. "If it had not been for Simon, you would not be here. If it had not been for his choices, I would not have met you."

"And if it is a girl?"

"What would like to name her?"

"I should like to call her Marian, after your mother."

Tears shone in his eyes, but he blinked them back as he stared at her. "How did I get so lucky?"

"You?" She went up on her elbows. "I am the lucky one. I would not have made it in this world had it not been for you."

He nuzzled his face against her belly, kissing her there before pulling her into his arms, where he showed her exactly how much he loved her.

Why an electronic book?

We live in the Information Age—an exciting time in the history of human civilization, in which technology rules supreme and continues to progress in leaps and bounds every minute of every day. For a multitude of reasons, more and more avid literary fans are opting to purchase e-books instead of paper books. The question from those not yet initiated into the world of electronic reading is simply: *Why?*

1. *Price.* An electronic title at Ellora's Cave Publishing and Cerridwen Press runs anywhere from 40% to 75% less than the cover price of the exact same title in paperback format. Why? Basic mathematics and cost. It is less expensive to publish an e-book (no paper and printing, no warehousing and shipping) than it is to publish a paperback, so the savings are passed along to the consumer.

2. *Space.* Running out of room in your house for your books? That is one worry you will never have with electronic books. For a low one-time cost, you can purchase a handheld device specifically designed for e-reading. Many e-readers have large, convenient screens for viewing. Better yet, hundreds of titles can be stored within your new library—on a single microchip. There are a variety of e-readers from different manufacturers. You can also read e-books

on your PC or laptop computer. (Please note that Ellora's Cave does not endorse any specific brands. You can check our websites at www.ellorascave.com or www.cerridwenpress.com for information we make available to new consumers.)

3. *Mobility.* Because your new e-library consists of only a microchip within a small, easily transportable e-reader, your entire cache of books can be taken with you wherever you go.

4. *Personal Viewing Preferences.* Are the words you are currently reading too small? Too large? Too… ANNOYING? Paperback books cannot be modified according to personal preferences, but e-books can.

5. *Instant Gratification.* Is it the middle of the night and all the bookstores near you are closed? Are you tired of waiting days, sometimes weeks, for bookstores to ship the novels you bought? Ellora's Cave Publishing sells instantaneous downloads twenty-four hours a day, seven days a week, every day of the year. Our webstore is never closed. Our e-book delivery system is 100% automated, meaning your order is filled as soon as you pay for it.

Those are a few of the top reasons why electronic books are replacing paperbacks for many avid readers.

As always, Ellora's Cave and Cerridwen Press welcome your questions and comments. We invite you to email us at Comments@ellorascave.com or write to us directly at Ellora's Cave Publishing Inc., 1056 Home Avenue, Akron, OH 44310-3502.

erridwen, the Celtic Goddess of wisdom, was the muse who brought inspiration to storytellers and those in the creative arts. Cerridwen Press encompasses the best and most innovative stories in all genres of today's fiction. Visit our site and discover the newest titles by talented authors who still get inspired - much like the ancient storytellers did, once upon a time.

Cerridwen Press

www.cerridwenpress.com

CERRIDWEN PRESS

Cerridwen, the Celtic goddess of wisdom, was the muse who brought inspiration to storytellers and those in the creative arts.

Cerridwen Press encompasses the best and most innovative stories in all genres of today's fiction.

Visit our website and discover the newest titles by talented authors who still get inspired — much like the ancient storytellers did…

once upon a time.

www.cerridwenpress.com

Made in the USA